RUGBY ACADEMY

TOM PALMER

Conkers

onkers

First published in 2019 in Great Britain by
Barrington Stoke Ltd
18 Walker Street, Edinburgh, EH3 7LP

www.barringtonstoke.co.uk

Text © 2014, 2015 Tom Palmer
Illustrations © 2014, 2015 David Shephard

A CIP catalogue record for this book is available
from the British Library upon request

ISBN: 978-1-78112-866-4

Printed and bound by CPI Group (UK) Ltd, Croydon, CR0 4YY

For Jane Walker

CONTENTS

1

COMBAT ZONE

ONE

The silver BMW made a sharp swerve left to avoid the deer that stood frozen in its headlights. Woody held his breath. A part of him wished the car had come off the road. But only so that the journey would stop – he didn't have a death wish or anything like that.

But the car didn't come off the road. Woody watched his dad's arms tense as he controlled the car with perfect skill. That was how Woody's dad always drove. It was part of who he was.

A man who liked to travel at speed.

A fighter pilot in the RAF.

Woody stared out of the car window. Its headlights lit up the forest on either side of the road. Thick tree trunks flashed by.

"I don't want to do this," Woody said. "I liked my old school. I liked my friends. I'm just about to start my GCSEs."

His dad didn't take his eyes from the road. "Borderlands is a great school," he said. "It was my school. You'll make new friends. You'll play lots of sport."

"The wrong sport," Woody snapped.

His dad paused before he spoke again. Woody knew he was working out what to say so that he could win the argument.

"Rugby is a wonderful game," his dad said at last. "I learned more from rugby than you'll ever learn playing soccer. And the school runs a serious rugby academy now."

"It's called football," Woody said. "And I like football. I'm good at football. You know I am."

Woody's dad was silent again. They were out of the forest now. The BMW was speeding up a winding slope onto a moor.

Woody thought about the letter he had received a month before from Norwich City. They'd offered him a place in their football academy. That was the reason his dad was driving him to Borderlands – to stop him being a footballer. Woody had even had to hide his football in his bag so his dad didn't know he'd taken it with him.

"There's more to life than sport," his dad went on. "You'll get a better education at Borderlands. It's a fine school. One of the best."

Woody didn't reply. He wanted to swear at his dad like his dad swore when he was angry. But Woody kept his anger locked deep inside himself.

It was at times like this that he wished his mum was still around. She always knew how to break the tension. But she was in Australia. Remarried with two new daughters. Woody had made the choice to stay in England with his dad.

After a few minutes of tense silence, Woody's dad switched on the radio. The news headlines filled the car.

Floods in Cornwall and Devon.

The Man U manager had been sacked.

Then back to the main story.

"There have been further scenes of violent conflict in the Central Asian Republic," the reporter said. "The Prime Minister is on his way to New York to speak at the United Nations. Before he left, he said, 'We must take this situation seriously. It threatens the peace of the whole Middle East. We must do what we can for the people of the Central

Asian Republic.' Experts predict that the UK will be at war within 24 hours."

Woody saw his dad's hands tighten their grip on the steering wheel.

TWO

"Wow!" Woody's mouth fell open. He couldn't help it. He'd seen photos of his dad's old school, but it still took his breath away in real life.

It was nothing like Woody's last school. That didn't have a high stone wall all around it. It didn't have a mile-long, tree-lined drive leading to its front door either. But what struck Woody most was in front of the school, in pride of place. A rugby field, lit up by four massive floodlights. On the pitch behind it he saw 20 or so boys in blue and yellow striped shirts.

"That's Luxton Park. The hallowed turf," Woody's dad said. "Magnificent, isn't it?"

"It's very nice, Dad," Woody said. He had decided not to argue any more. In the three minutes it had taken to travel up the school drive, he'd made a plan. A plan that would solve all his problems.

Woody's dad smiled as he parked in front of the school.

"This brings back memories," he said.

"Yeah?"

"Oh yes." Woody's dad leaned back in his seat to stretch his back and shoulders. "Of course, your grandad sent me up on the train."

As they spoke, a light came on outside the school and a man appeared at the car window.

"Flight Officer Woodward?" the man said. "We've been expecting you. I'm Mr Clayton."

Mr Clayton was a little older than Woody's dad. He had short dark hair that was just turning grey.

"Good evening," Woody's dad said. "This is—"

"I get called Woody," Woody said.

"Hello, Woody," Mr Clayton said. "I'm going to be your housemaster at Borderlands. I'm here to help you with anything and everything."

"Thank you," Woody said.

"May I speak to your father for a moment?"

Woody nodded. His dad got out of the car, giving Woody a chance to look at a road map in the door pocket. He tried to listen in on what his dad and Mr Clayton were saying, but the sound of dozens of rugby boots on concrete drowned their words out.

After a couple of minutes, Woody's dad signalled to Woody to get out of the car.

"Right. I'll be off," he announced. "Long drive back to Lincolnshire."

"See you, Dad," Woody said with a grin. He could tell his dad was surprised that he was so calm about being left at Borderlands. But it was clear he was pleased too – he had never been fond of goodbyes.

Of course, he didn't know about Woody's plan.

Mr Clayton led Woody down a wood-panelled corridor and across a stone courtyard into another building.

"You're sharing a room with two other boys," he explained. "Owen and Rory. Nice lads. They're keen on rugby too."

"Thank you," Woody said. He didn't see much reason to point out that he wasn't keen on rugby.

"And I meant what I told you," Mr Clayton said. "If I can help you with anything, please say."

Mr Clayton knocked on a door, then led Woody into the room, where two boys were sitting on their beds. One was reading. The other was typing on a laptop. They both jumped up and grinned.

When the housemaster had gone, Owen put the kettle on.

"What did you bring?" he asked. "We've got hot chocolate and biscuits. Want some? I'll make it while you unpack."

Woody nodded. "Yes, please," he said. He knew he needed to take on as much food as he could – it was going to be a long night. He also knew he wasn't going to unpack.

After they'd drunk their hot chocolate and eaten two packets of biscuits, Woody decided to tell Owen and Rory his plan. They were getting on well and he felt it would be wrong not to. He couldn't just disappear. He felt kind of sad he would only know the two boys for the next hour or two.

"Listen," he said. "I'm planning to leave tonight."

"Leave?" Owen stared at him.

Woody explained his plan to run across the hills

to a train station about 14 miles away. He'd checked the map in the car. He'd sleep in the station for the rest of the night, get the first train to Birmingham in the morning, then head on to Lincolnshire.

"But won't your dad just bring you back?" Rory asked.

Woody shook his head. "I think he'll understand that I'm not happy. If I'm home by breakfast."

THREE

Woody waited until midnight before he set off.

All that he had with him was a small rucksack with a change of clothes, a bottle of water and another packet of biscuits that Rory had given him.

He jogged across the school rugby pitch, warming his legs up for a long night of running. But then he was surprised by a beam of light that came from behind him and swept across the grass.

On instinct, he speeded up into a sprint.

"Hey! I can see you out there," a voice shouted. "Keep off our property. This is a school, not a public park. I'm releasing the dog."

A bark. A rush of adrenaline. Woody ran harder.

The high stone wall was right ahead. Woody sprinted towards it, not convinced he could scale it. The drop on the other side would be well over two metres.

But Woody had no choice. If he didn't get over the wall, he'd get bitten by the dog, and his escape attempt would be over. He ran. Hard. He made the wall, scaled it, lay on the top, then dropped down as softly as he could.

Woody landed on both feet, bending his knees. He paused and held his breath. It was OK. A safe landing. No more sounds of man or dog.

Now to run into the hills.

The night was dark away from Borderlands, but Woody knew which road to follow – it was the same one his dad had driven him along. The run out of the town and up the valley was fine. Woody had done night-running along the river at home and he was used to the sounds of the night as he ran. But up on the moors it was different. The sky was huge, filled with a million pinprick stars. And it was quiet. Woody felt lonely and small in that huge open space. He couldn't help but wonder if this was how his dad felt when he was alone in his plane in the night sky.

The rest of the night went to plan. But when Woody got off the train in his home town at 8.30 the next morning, he noticed that there were more fighter aircraft in the sky than he had ever seen before. Tiny silver reflections of sunlight high above the miles upon miles of the flat fields of Lincolnshire.

A Typhoon took off from the airbase, its engines firing, the air vibrating.

But perhaps this was normal. When the British Prime Minister was at the United Nations, the RAF would step up their training. It looked good on the news. It sent the message that the UK was ready to send its air force into action.

Woody walked along the lane to his home, hands in pockets, lost in thought. At the front door he knocked, rather than letting himself into the house and giving his dad a fright.

There was no reply.

And Woody realised that something didn't feel right. His dad always did the same things at the same time, and right now he should be out of the shower, eating his breakfast, hungry after his morning run. Then Woody noticed the BMW wasn't in the garage. And the bins were out in the road, even though it wasn't bin day.

Woody fished his iPhone out of his rucksack. There was a message:

Woody. We've been mobilised. Short notice.

I'll phone when I can. Try to enjoy school.

Love Dad

Woody sat down on the doorstep. Then he threw up.

When he had recovered, Woody flicked through the BBC News app on his phone.

The Prime Minister was back in the UK. Parliament would vote that day on whether to go to war to secure the stability of the Central Asian Republic. Woody knew what would happen. They would vote yes.

The rest of the world might not know there was going to be a war, but the RAF was already on its way.

FOUR

Back at Borderlands, Woody was sitting on his bed when the door to the dorm burst open. It was Owen and Rory, both in blue and yellow tops and covered in mud.

Rory came over, put his rugby ball on the floor and shook Woody's hand. Then he picked the ball back up and began to collect flecks of cut grass off the carpet, one by one.

"Training," Owen explained. "First XV."

"Right," Woody said.

"How was the escape?" Owen asked.

Woody smiled. "I made it all the way home."

"How was your dad?" Rory asked.

Woody wasn't sure what to say, and for a moment the three boys looked at each other in uncomfortable silence. Then Rory spotted the pack of blueys on Woody's bed – official RAF postcards families could send to personnel who were away in combat.

Rory screwed up his face. "I'm sorry. He's gone, hasn't he?"

A wave of panic stopped Woody from speaking. It was the same panic he'd felt on the step at home. He took a deep breath and looked out of the window at a groundsman who was replacing divots on the rugby pitch.

"David's dad's gone too," Owen said. "You've not met David yet. And Jesse – he's David's mate – his dad's an Air Marshal. He's gone too. There are quite a few boys here whose parents have gone."

Woody had been ten the last time his dad had been deployed. Back then, it had been exciting. His dad was a fighter pilot. One of the best airmen in the world. His mum had been at home then, and she had helped him to stay positive about the fact his dad was gone. Woody had been proud, not worried about what could go wrong. Now he'd prefer it if his dad was a groundsman, like the one outside.

"Listen," Owen said. "We're going to watch the match now. Rory's got an Australian pay-TV channel. Australia's playing New Zealand. Want to watch it with us?"

Woody nodded. It was a good plan. A way of not having to talk.

Australia against New Zealand was a fierce encounter. The two teams battered each other from kick-off. An Australian was taken off for a bleeding cut after 8 minutes. A Kiwi after 12.

Woody watched with mixed feelings. He loved to see players running hard with the ball, smashing through a tackle, or being brought down. But the scrums sent a shiver up his spine. Anything could happen in that pile of bodies. He watched as a huge man was dragged under a scrum. He was two metres tall at least, but still he ended up tipped up so that his legs were in the air.

It reminded Woody of a player he'd seen at a match once with his dad at their local ground. The scrum had collapsed and when everyone stood back up, one man was still lying there. He was carried off the pitch on a stretcher.

Woody had only been five at the time and he'd thought the player had died and was being taken away to be put in a coffin. It had worried him so much that he couldn't get to sleep that night, so he'd gone into his parents' room to ask his dad about it.

His dad said the man was only knocked out, not dead.

From then on, Woody had never wanted to play rugby. He couldn't shake off the chill of fear he'd felt as a five-year-old boy.

But he said nothing about that to Owen and Rory. He just drank his Coke and – he had to be honest with himself – kind of enjoyed the match.

FIVE

"Do you fancy a school tour now you're staying?" Rory asked.

"OK," Woody said. "You're on."

Owen, Rory and Woody walked down endless corridors, past classrooms, a dining hall and random piles of sports kit. Owen introduced Woody to several other boys as they walked. Most were friendly and shook Woody's hand.

But then he met two Borderlands pupils who weren't friendly in the least. A tall boy with light hair and a sneer, and his shorter, stockier friend.

"Who's this?" the light-haired boy asked Owen.

"This is Woody," Owen said in a guarded tone. "Woody, this is Jesse and David."

"Hi," Woody said, and put his hand out.

There was a moment of silence. Then Jesse and David just walked on down the corridor.

Woody was confused. He rubbed his forehead. "What's their problem?" he asked.

"They're tricky," Owen replied. "Especially Jesse. He's worth keeping an eye out for."

"What do you mean?" Woody asked.

"He can be ..." Rory hesitated. "Difficult."

Woody tried to look like he understood, but he didn't. They reached a common room next. A big TV was on showing the news. Woody felt compelled to watch.

The reporter was saying that the RAF was already over the Central Asian Republic, where they could monitor developments in the troubled country. And Typhoons were moving in from Cyprus, ready to attack if needed.

Woody shuddered. The thought of his dad in his Typhoon made him shake with fear. Fear that he might be called into action like he had been over Iraq, Afghanistan and Libya. He hated the idea. His dad alone in a red-hot sky, while surface-to-air missiles rocketed towards him.

"Good evening, boys."

The voice at the door made the boys jump. A female voice. The head teacher, Mrs Page.

Owen, Rory and Woody stood up straight away, as did several other boys. Someone pressed mute on the TV remote control. This was the first time Woody had seen the head teacher up close. She looked like she meant business in her smart trouser suit. Mr Clayton was with her.

"I know you boys have an interest in the war," Mrs Page said. "But don't watch too much of it on the news. The reporters' job isn't just to inform their viewers, it's also to entertain them. And that means they don't always stick to the truth. Do you understand?"

"Yes, miss," Rory and Owen said.

"I hope you're settling in, Woodward?" Mrs Page asked.

"Er ... yes, miss." Woody felt himself blushing under the head teacher's gaze. Did she know about last night? His escape?

"Woodward is settling in very well," Mr Clayton said.

"Good." Mrs Page turned to leave. "And remember what I said about the TV news, boys."

"Yes, miss," Woody said again.

When Mrs Page had gone, Woody nodded to Mr Clayton. "Thank you," he said. "I owe you a favour, sir."

"Indeed you do." Mr Clayton rubbed his hands

together. "Which is good, because I need one."

Woody smiled and waited to hear what Mr Clayton wanted from him.

"Mr Johnson is short of players," Mr Clayton said. "He needs backs. And you look like a back to me, Woody."

"A back as in rugby, sir?" Woody asked.

"Yes, rugby," Mr Clayton said. He picked up the remote and switched off the TV. "Mr Johnson is the rugby master and I think it's time you met him."

SIX

"What do you do after dinner?" Woody asked as he and Owen and Rory walked away from the dining hall later that evening.

"Homework," Owen replied. "I'm going to the library. It's quiet now. Miss Evans will be there on her own."

"I'll come with you," Woody said. "I need a library right now."

Rory tapped each wooden panel as they walked along the corridor. Woody didn't comment on it. He was getting used to Rory's funny habits.

"I need to practise kicking," Rory said. "Before it gets dark."

Rory disappeared down a corridor to the pitches outside, and Woody and Owen walked on to the library. Owen took Woody in and they went up to the desk.

"This is Woody," Owen said. "He needs some help."

"Great. Hello, Woody – I'm Miss Evans," the librarian said. "What can I do to help?"

Woody looked at Miss Evans. She had bright, happy-looking eyes and was wearing a Welsh rugby top. *Is everyone in this school obsessed with rugby?* he thought. But he kept his thoughts to himself.

"I need a book on the rules of rugby, please," Woody said.

Miss Evans led Woody to the sports books. He was surprised to see a whole shelf of books on how to play rugby.

"There are loads," he said. "I never thought there'd be so many."

"There *are* loads," Miss Evans agreed. "And they're all useful. But you want this one."

Woody took the book. It was called *Know the Game: Rugby Union*. He hoped it did what it said on the cover. He loved sport, but he still felt reluctant to play rugby. Very reluctant. But he had made Mr Clayton a promise. And he reckoned it was a promise the housemaster wouldn't let him break.

Woody found a comfy seat and opened the book.

He read about the dimensions of a Rugby Union pitch. The size of the ball. The positions of the players. Forwards in the scrum. Backs lined out behind them.

Woody frowned. He'd always thought the backs went in the scrum. He had a lot to learn.

As Woody read, he heard the library door open

and close and random footsteps come in and out, but he was too engrossed to look up. Miss Evans had been right about this book. Now he was reading about ways to score. Five points for a try. Two for a conversion. Three for a drop goal or penalty.

All of a sudden there was a hand on the table in front of him. Knuckles white, nails bitten down.

Woody looked up and saw Jesse and David looming over him.

"What's that you're reading?" Jesse asked.

"It's a book about rugby." Woody knew the boys weren't being friendly, but he grinned at them anyway.

Jesse smiled a nasty smile. "A book about rugby? Are you serious?"

Woody did his best to smile again. But he said nothing.

"That's the kind of thing I'd expect David's kid

sister to do," Jesse went on. "You don't learn about rugby in a book. You learn it on the pitch."

Woody looked at David. Now he looked angry with Jesse. Owen hadn't been kidding when he said Jesse was difficult.

SEVEN

Woody had never felt so awkward. A gum shield was pushing his lips out and he had a scrum cap squashing his head. Rugby gear. He'd never needed all this stuff to play football. It made him worry even more about getting hurt. But he had a promise to keep.

Woody stuck close to Rory and Owen, who led him to a pitch on the far side of the school grounds.

"Why aren't we training on there?" Woody asked, looking across at Luxton Park. He'd been looking forward to telling his dad he'd played on the "hallowed turf".

Owen laughed and looked at Rory. "If you go on there, Mr Johnson will have to kill you."

"What?"

"First XV games only. Nobody else is allowed on there – except the groundsman."

Woody shook his head. This school was weird.

A giant of a man was leading the training, assisted by another man who had a permanent scowl.

Owen and Rory told Woody who the coaches were as they walked over towards them. The giant was the chief coach, Mr Johnson. The scowler was his assistant, Mr Searle. Woody also noticed three figures passing fast balls to one another at close range. Jesse, David and another boy, Thomas. Owen had introduced Woody to him earlier.

The sight of Jesse made Woody feel even more uneasy. He watched Jesse as he spoke to the other two and pointed at Woody. All three of them started laughing. Woody felt a heat run up the back of his neck into his head. He knew this feeling – it was anger. The same as his dad's anger. His dad's voice came to him – "Always channel the red mist, Woody."

Woody decided to follow his dad's advice. He had his anger. He had his worries about rugby. He had his fears for his dad. And he needed a way to channel those angers and fears that didn't involve running away again. He'd do it by throwing himself into the game.

Training began – under floodlights while a halo of rain drifted across the pitch.

First they jogged the lengths of the pitch and then, once they were warmed up, they sprinted widths. Woody made sure he finished ahead of everyone else at each sprint. He might not know how to play rugby, but he did know how to run.

Next they practised passing in lines up and down the pitch. After one length of the pitch, Mr Johnson stopped the session and walked up to Woody.

"Spin it," he said.

"Sorry, sir?"

"The ball. When you pass, spin it." The coach gave the ball back to Woody. "I'm Mr Johnson," he said. "You must be Woodward?"

"I am, sir."

"He's not got to the bit in the book about passing yet," Woody heard Jesse shout over.

Mr Johnson looked at Jesse, then Woody, waiting for someone to explain.

"I've not played much rugby," Woody admitted. "I don't know how to spin the ball."

Mr Johnson nodded, then showed Woody what to do. "If you spin it," he explained, "the ball will travel further and you can control it better."

Then he jogged backwards and tossed the ball to Woody. Woody saw the ball spinning as it moved in a straight line towards him. He tossed it back, trying to spin it too. After three or four goes, he started to feel like he had control of the ball.

"Good," Mr Johnson said. "You're a natural."

After passing, they worked on charging.

One boy took the ball from a short pass, then ran at another two boys, who were holding blue and yellow tackle pads. The idea was for the attacker to make ground by hitting the defenders hard.

Woody stood in line. As he waited, he tried to spin the ball, practising what Mr Johnson had shown him, tossing it upwards.

"Spinning the ball is on page 32 of *Rugby for Idiots*," Woody heard Jesse say in a slow, stupid-sounding voice.

One or two other boys laughed.

Woody felt his anger rising again just as it was his turn to go.

He tossed the ball to Mr Johnson, then began to run, taking a short pass back from the coach. Then he accelerated. Fast. He charged at three boys with yellow and blue pads. He hit them. Hard. Really hard. It hurt – for a second. Then there was a rush of adrenaline and he felt the defenders give to the weight of his shoulder. It felt good.

After training, Mr Johnson walked alongside Woody. He was at least a head taller than Woody and twice as wide across the shoulders. Both his ears stuck out like he'd spent a lifetime in the scrum.

"Fast, aren't you?" he asked.

"I suppose," Woody said.

"You've not played rugby before?"

"Football. I was a centre forward." Woody wondered if he should say that Norwich City wanted him, but he decided he would sound like he was showing off if he did.

"At a high level, I bet?" the coach said. "Your acceleration is remarkable."

"Thank you, sir," Woody said.

"Listen," Mr Johnson said. "We've lost a couple of lads. Brothers. Backs. I might be able to use you in the teams. If we trained you up."

Woody nodded.

"You'd need to put in a lot of work," Mr Johnson warned.

Woody thought of his dad. How funny it would be to tell him that he was in one of the rugby teams at school. And that he had even enjoyed the training session.

"I'll put the work in," Woody said. "Sir."

EIGHT

Woody's iPad flashed to Skype just after he'd got into bed and picked up his rugby book.

His dad. He felt a rush of excitement.

"Dad! How are you? Where are you?"

"Fine, son. How's Borderlands?"

Woody understood. His dad couldn't answer his questions. He wasn't allowed to say anything about where he was and what he was doing. There was a war on – and he was fighting in it.

"Great," Woody said.

He watched his dad's face relax.

"Friends?" he asked.

"I'm in with two lads," Woody told him. "They're sound."

Woody glanced at his room-mates. Rory was scribbling in a notebook. Owen was on his Xbox.

"How's the schoolwork?" Dad asked.

"Not done much yet," Woody said. "But I'm on the team."

"Oh, don't tell me they play soccer now," his dad sighed. "That's the end."

"Rugby, Dad."

"What?"

"I did rugby training. It went well. The coach wants to work with me."

His dad looked stunned. Woody felt a wave of happiness, then sadness. He didn't want to give in to his confused feelings, so he fired another question at his dad.

"How's the war?"

"You know I can't talk about it, Wood. I'm fine. Busy. I only have another minute or two."

"I know," Woody said. That was how these calls always were. Short. Intense. Unsatisfying.

"Look, I've been worried," Dad went on. "The way I bundled you off to Borderlands. So, I wanted to make you a deal. To make it easier while you're there and I'm here."

"Go on."

"You throw yourself into it there – enjoy it – and when I get back we'll talk about where you want to be. OK?"

"That sounds fair," Woody said. "It's a deal."

He knew his dad was worried. But he also knew his dad had to give his job 100%. A fighter pilot couldn't be worrying about his son and if he liked his school or not. He needed all his focus to survive. But, still, Woody couldn't resist one last question.

"And we'll talk about what sport I want to play?" he asked.

There was a pause.

Then his dad smiled and said, "Yes, that too."

An hour later, Woody was outside in the courtyard. It was raining, and he was pleased. He was less likely to be disturbed in the rain.

He dropped his football on the stone slabs and trapped it. For a moment he didn't kick it. He was thinking about what his dad was doing now. Woody imagined him putting his flying gear on, his helmet, then walking across the runway to his plane. He would check the aircraft's wings, wheels, cannons – and then climb in.

Woody stopped imagining there and fired the football hard at a wall. It bounced back and he left-foot controlled it, then hit it with his right. He did this over and over, harder and harder, till sweat ran down his back. The effort felt really good. The more he put in, the less he had to think about his dad. About anything. Woody didn't want to think at all. Just kick, kick, kick.

"HEY YOU!" The voice was sharp and loud.

Woody trapped his football and turned round. Mr Searle was at the door, hands on hips. Woody watched him, unsure of what to do.

"Give me that ball," Mr Searle demanded.

Woody flicked the ball up with his instep, walked over to the coach and handed it to him.

"You're new, so I'll let this go," Mr Searle growled. "But this is a rugby school. No soccer balls." Then he turned and marched towards the sports building, the football under his arm.

Woody felt a flash of rage. What about his ball?

"When do I get the ball back?" Woody shouted. "SIR?"

"You don't," Mr Searle said, not looking round.

No way!

How unfair could you get?

Woody watched Mr Searle go in a door and a light come on. He heard excited yapping. It was the dog from the night he tried to escape. Of course – it had been Mr Searle with the torch that night.

Woody approached and peered in through a metal grille at a window. He could see Mr Searle with the football in one hand. And in the other hand a pair of shears. Woody watched him put the ball on the ground, lift the shears high, then plunge them down to stab the football. The dog was leaping around the room, barking and snapping. Finally, Mr Searle threw the punctured ball to the dog. It set on it as if it was a small animal to kill.

Now Woody's anger was off the scale.

But he could do nothing. Not to the dog. Not to Mr Searle. So he ran. Across Luxton Park, then around the perimeter wall. He would run until he was sick or he collapsed. He felt the strain in his legs first. Then his lungs. And then the feeling of power began to overcome his anger.

NINE

A couple of weeks passed. Woody did Maths, English, even Latin. He tried hard and kept out of trouble. He was aware that the school would report back to parents about boys' progress. Woody didn't want his dad to think that he was going back on their deal. He would tolerate Borderlands until the war was over.

In the Central Asian Republic, British planes were still bombing rebel air fields, defences and other key targets. The south of the country and its borders were safe now and the RAF was turning its attention to the north. This meant more danger for pilots like Woody's dad.

On the rugby field, Woody threw himself into every training session. He went out at other times with Owen and Rory to practise his skills. He had overcome his fear of hurting himself.

Yes, you fell over.

Yes, you bashed into people or they bashed into you.

Yes, other boys piled on top of you and pushed you this way and that.

But you came out laughing rather than crying. The pain you felt on impact gave way fast to adrenaline and the thrill of being part of a team. It felt good to be playing a sport that involved something close to wrestling, using your strength and your skill to get the better of someone else. Woody liked it – and he thought he was pretty good at it too.

And Mr Johnson was happy with him.

During one practice game, Woody made Mr Johnson even happier. It was the First XV versus the Second XV. A warm-up for the Firsts, who were due to play a semi-final in a week's time. And not just any semi-final – the semi-final of the National Schools Trophy. Even Woody knew that it was a big deal.

Woody was in the Seconds.

Twenty minutes into the game, Woody ran from deep, built up pace and received the ball from the scrum half. He wanted to gain a few metres, get closer to the line, and he charged. As he accelerated, he saw no gap between the First XV backs. It was a solid line of boys. So Woody did something he'd read about in his rugby books. He dropped the ball, tapped a grubber kick low, then ran at the First XV line. And all of a sudden he was in space, on his own, un-tackled. The ball bounced ahead of him, the

defence were behind him. He kicked it again, over the 22-metre line.

Woody ran at pace, his lungs and legs working hard. Another kick. Softer this time. He saw the ball bounce once, then twice, then it reared up just before the try line. Woody dived after it, his arms at full stretch.

Contact.

A try.

Woody's first ever try. It felt great, brilliant – nothing like scoring a goal in football. To be on the end of a move, to battle your way past all those other players who were trying to stop you, and then to dive down to put the ball over the line. It made Woody feel like he wanted more. To train and practise and compete as hard as he could, to have that feeling again.

After training, Mr Johnson took Woody aside. "You're doing well," he said. "Very well."

"Thank you, sir."

"I want to take you to the semi-final," Mr Johnson said. "On the bench. Can you cope with that?"

Woody was stunned. Was Mr Johnson really asking him to play for Borderlands in the National Schools Trophy? For the Firsts?

"Am I experienced enough, sir?" he said in disbelief.

Mr Johnson grinned at him. "No."

"Oh," Woody said. He didn't know whether to grin back.

"But I can use you," Mr Johnson told him. "As an impact player. You're a natural sportsman. OK?"

Woody just about managed to say, "Yes."

TEN

When the minibus turned onto the drive of Thornton School in Yorkshire, Woody's heart started to pound.

Until then he had managed to distract himself by joking about with some of the other boys and listening to loud music, but now the scale of what was about to happen struck him.

He was on the bench in a rugby game. A high-stakes rugby game. If Borderlands won this game, then they were in the final of the National Schools Trophy.

When Mr Johnson stopped the bus at the top of the school drive, nobody spoke or moved. There was no messing about or pushing to get off. Woody knew it was time for a team talk.

"First of all," Mr Johnson said, "I want you to remember that you represent Borderlands. In everything you do, on and off the field. You will be polite. You will be sporting. You will be grateful. You will be helpful. OK?"

"Yes, sir," they said.

"Second," Mr Johnson went on. "You do everything you can to win this game. Play within the rules, but remember you are 80 minutes away from the final at Twickenham, the home of English rugby. Do you want that?"

"Yes," a few boys said.

"I'm sorry?" Mr Johnson yelled.

"YES!" the whole squad shouted. The minibus shook to the sound of their voices.

*

The match was tight. The game was locked in the middle third of the muddy pitch. Woody found it hard to tell his own squad from the other team's players for the mud.

Two things struck him, sitting so close to the action. One was the smell of the mud. He could really smell it. It reminded him of playing football in the wet. The other was the shouting. Both sets of players – and their coaches – shouted to each other, worked as a unit, communicated non-stop. Woody liked it. And he wanted to be part of it.

Halfway through the second half, the score was 12–12. Four penalties to each team. No tries. Rory had scored four out of his four kicks. The Thornton fly half had scored four from seven.

One boy who was easy to spot was Jesse. He was superb. He dominated the game from scrum half, feeding players the ball, then taking it back, side-stepping tackles. He was an amazing rugby player.

But Woody could see, too, that Borderlands were getting tired. Thornton were gaining more and more ground, which meant they were within kicking distance of the posts if they were to try for a drop goal or if Borderlands gave them a penalty. Woody felt pleased with himself – he was learning to read the game.

Just then he felt a tap on his back. Mr Johnson.

"Warm up," the coach said.

"What?" Woody asked, startled.

"Start warming up," Mr Johnson said. "You're going on in five."

Borderlands had just won a scrum when Woody was sent onto the pitch. He took up position at centre, 15 metres left of Jesse.

At first, Woody struggled to take in the game

around him. He knew he had to focus, work with the rest of the team, not give in to his feelings of anxiety. Jesse, hands on the ball, gave Woody a hard stare.

"Watch me," Jesse shouted. "Do what I say. Get the ball to Thomas, to Owen. And listen to the others. Got it?"

"Got it," Woody shouted back.

But Woody had other orders from Mr Johnson. When the ball was fed out to him, he was to run at the Thornton defence. He was to gather pace and hit them hard. Use his power and size to batter them. He was to gain ground by running at and through Thornton.

Woody spotted Thornton's captain shouting at his backs and pointing at Woody. They were wary of him. His fresh legs. The determination on his face. They didn't know he was as green as a rugby player comes.

Jesse fed the ball into the scrum. Seconds later it came out of the back. Jesse waited as the two sets of players pushed at each other. Then he picked the ball up and passed it across the field.

Woody saw the ball come through three sets of hands – Jesse, Thomas and Owen – as the Thornton backs pressed. He had chosen to stay far back to give himself the chance to build momentum with his run. So when the ball came to him he was already running fast. He took it two-handed and close to his side and ran low and hard at the defence. He pushed a hand into the face of his first tackler, deflecting him. Then two players hit him at the same time – one on his legs, one round his hips. Woody crashed to the ground. He'd made seven metres. He turned over and held the ball behind him. Jesse was there, ready to take it.

The last ten minutes of the match felt like an hour to Woody. Every time he got the ball, he did as the coach had told him. Gathered pace. Gained ground. Hit the defence hard. And he did it time after time.

Now Borderlands were making ground. They were less vulnerable to penalties and drop goals. Mr Johnson's plan was working.

The score remained at 12–12.

Woody did his best to put a little bit more into each of his charges. To get stronger with each, not weaker. On his 8th charge, one of the other team grabbed him around the neck. The referee's whistle went straight away. High tackle. Dangerous play.

Woody stood when he was free of the heap of bodies that had fallen on top of him. He could see that Rory was holding the ball, eyeing the goals.

The Borderlands team backed off as Rory lined up the kick. The players and the small crowd went quiet. There was just the sound of a flag flapping in the wind. Rory stepped up, moved back two paces, one sideward, his eyes on the posts, then the ball, then the posts again.

One step. Two steps. The sound of boot on ball as it sailed between the posts. Dead centre. Perfect.

Thornton 12. Borderlands 15.

ELEVEN

Borderlands had won. They were in the final of the National Schools Trophy. At Twickenham. It was beyond belief.

The mood on the minibus was upbeat and excited. Thornton School had given them a huge hamper of cans of Coke, sandwiches, cakes and fruit for the journey home.

They ate. They drank. They talked. They laughed. They lived every move and kick of the game again and again.

After an hour, half the boys were bursting for the toilet and the rest wanted to stretch their legs after the game. Their muscles were stiffening, every minor injury nagging.

"Are we nearly there yet?" David joked. He got a few laughs, led by Jesse.

They were halfway across a moor, in the middle of nowhere. Mr Johnson parked the minibus.

"Let's stop here for five minutes, lads," he said. "Take a comfort break. Do some stretching."

Woody heard the minibus radio playing Nirvana as he stumbled in the dark, away from the bus. He stretched his legs and his back as he walked. His shoulders were sore and bruised. But it felt good, like war wounds. He'd earned them.

Then the music stopped. There were voices on the radio now. Woody approached a cluster of his team-mates around the minibus. They all stood in silence.

"What's up?" Woody called out.

"Shhhhh," Owen hissed.

Woody felt his stomach lurch.

"The RAF has made a number of successful strikes around the city of Lusa today," the reporter was saying. "Pairs of Tornados and Typhoons attacked rebel positions while, on the ground ..."

Woody swallowed. Typhoons. This was not how he wanted to hear news about the war. He wanted to be in his room, on his own, so that he could think properly.

"In a separate action in the south of the Central Asian Republic, a British Hercules aircraft has been reported missing," the reporter went on. "The aircraft was on a mission to rescue stranded British oil workers. First reports say it was shot down while attempting to land in the desert ..."

Woody noticed several boys fumble for their mobile phones. Their faces lit up on the dark hillside as they checked for messages.

"Come on, boys," Mr Johnson said. "Into the bus. Let's get back to school."

TWELVE

The first thing Woody did when he woke in the half light of the next morning was to check the BBC News app.

The RAF Hercules had crash-landed before it reached the stranded oil workers. It seemed almost certain that it had been shot down. RAF Search and Rescue had gone straight in and found all four of the crew. Three were injured. One had been killed. His family had been informed. The missions of the other RAF planes involved had been successful.

Woody closed his eyes. He hated this. He wished again that his dad did a nice safe job like a groundsman – anything other than a fighter pilot.

At breakfast, Woody could sense a gathering gloom. Boys sat at rows of tables with food in front of them, but no one was eating. No one was speaking.

When all the boarders and staff were in the dining hall, Mrs Page stood up. She cleared her throat. "Boys," she said. "We want to speak to you all together. To say this to every one of you."

Woody knew what was coming. The crew member killed on the Hercules. He was connected to Borderlands.

"David Henson left school early this morning," Mrs Page said. "His father was on board the Hercules that was shot down yesterday in the Central Asian Republic. I'm sorry to tell you that David's father was the crew member who was killed."

A couple of gasps.

Then silence.

Woody put his head in his hands. He'd imagined a thousand times how it might feel to be woken in the night to be told his own dad was missing or killed. It was unthinkable. Unspeakable. He wondered how David would be feeling now. And he had a sister, Woody remembered. How would she be feeling? And his mum? Woody couldn't even begin to imagine.

"Lessons will go on as normal," Mrs Page said into the silence. "Our thoughts are with David and his family. But it is best that school continues."

Woody worked his way through a bowl of cereal, surrounded by his school-mates. No one said a word. No one looked at anyone else. When he had finished, Woody went up to his dorm. He had ten minutes before form class.

He took out his iPad, sat by the window and called his dad on Skype. He knew there was no way his dad would be there. He knew there was no way his dad would answer. He would be working or sleeping.

Woody held his breath as Skype tried to connect.

There was no reply.

THIRTEEN

There was one week to go until the final of the National Schools Trophy. It was a cool night for another training session. Mr Johnson was driving the boys hard with complex passing drills and fitness work.

Woody found that he loved the intensity of rugby. He didn't have a fear of being hit any more – he wanted contact. There was nothing he enjoyed more than picking up his pace with the ball, trying to find a gap. If he was brought down, he just got up, ready to go again.

After training, Mr Johnson and Mr Searle asked

the boys to sit in a circle on the pitch. Steam rose above them as they sat and stretched their legs out in front of them. The floodlights from the pitch lit up some boys' faces and cast shadows across others.

"We've had a letter from Shadwell School," Mr Johnson said. "Our opponents in the final. It's something we need to talk about."

As Mr Johnson spoke, Woody noticed someone walking across the pitch towards them. The person looked ghostly with the lights of the school drive behind him.

"They've offered to forfeit the match." Mr Johnson paused. "To let us have the trophy uncontested." Another pause. "What do you think?"

"Accept," Jesse said. "Then we've won and we don't even have to show up. Who votes yes?"

Woody watched three or four hands go up.

Then a voice from behind the rugby coaches.

"Don't accept."

The team turned to see David standing there. He was back from his dad's funeral.

"David," Mr Johnson said. "Come and join us."

David walked into the centre of the circle.

"I heard what you were saying," he said. "About the letter, sir. We can't accept the offer. We have to play the final and win."

Woody watched David stare out into the dark. He'd stopped speaking. But nobody broke the silence.

"If we don't, it's like accepting we're weak," David said. "Because of what happened to my dad. Because we all know that's why they're offering to pull out. And we're not weak. We can't be weak."

FOURTEEN

"What's up, Rory?" Woody asked as he woke up with a start.

Rory was leaving the dorm with a ball under his arm and a notebook in his hand. It was dawn. The day before the final.

"Going kicking," Rory whispered.

"You never rest," Woody said.

"I'm awake," Owen muttered from under his duvet.

Rory shrugged, then smiled.

"Can I come?" Woody asked. "I'll field for you."

"Me too?" Owen asked, sitting up.

"OK," Rory said. "Be ready in five. Both of you."

Out on the pitch, Rory lined up six penalties. Six thumps of the ball. Six through the posts. Perfect.

Woody nodded to himself. He was impressed by Rory's skill, his dedication. Then he turned his mind to his own game. "Can we practise grubber kicks?" he asked. "I want to try something out."

"Sure," Rory agreed.

Woody tried a couple of times to break between Owen and Rory as they stood between him and the try line. But it didn't really work.

On his third attempt, Woody ended up running shoulder to shoulder with Owen, laughing, hoofing the ball towards the posts at the near end of Luxton Park.

Neither boy heard Rory's warning as Woody

pushed ahead of Owen to volley the ball underneath the posts, football style.

Woody heard barking first. Then a shout.

"YOU BOYS! GET OFF THE PARK! COME HERE!"

A volley of words, loud and hard. It could only be Mr Searle.

All three boys froze, their feet firmly on the out-of-bounds pitch.

When Mr Searle arrived, he snatched the ball from Owen.

"All three of you," he snapped. "Don't even start with the excuses. There's nothing you can say. Soccer on Luxton Park? I've never ... I can't ... You're all off the team. No final. No Twickenham. Get out of my sight. I need to speak to Mr Johnson right now."

Woody, Owen and Rory slouched back towards school. They had gone from the best of feelings to the worst. Now they felt nothing but shame and deep disappointment.

None of them spoke. What could they say?

FIFTEEN

It was the morning of the final, 24 hours later. There was a knock at the dorm door. The three boys groaned.

In the end, Woody answered it. He didn't want to face this. This was the day he was meant to play at Twickenham. The day he was going to make his dad proud. And he'd blown it.

Mr Johnson stood in the doorway. "The bus leaves at nine o'clock sharp," he said. "I want you on it. OK?"

The three boys stared at the coach. They'd not seen him since before the incident on Luxton Park. A summons to the team bus wasn't what they'd been expecting. They'd been expecting fury.

"OK?" the coach asked.

"Yes, sir," Woody, Owen and Rory said as one.

"I'll speak to Mr Searle. You think about the game. Sharpish. Do you want this or not?"

"We want it, sir!"

The bus was a proper coach, with decent heaters, a toilet and leg room. The team piled on, along with some of the teachers. Woody watched from the back seat. There was a lot to take in.

Mr Johnson was talking to a sullen Mr Searle.

David was sitting near the front, staring out stony-faced at the rain.

Jesse sat three rows away from his friend.

Woody tried to ignore his feelings towards Jesse and Mr Searle. If he let himself, he could get angry about them, but he didn't want to feel like that.

Woody wanted to focus on playing rugby. If he could get past everything he'd had to put up with in the last few days – as well as his anger – and just play rugby, that would be a victory in itself.

Twickenham towered over the school bus as it turned into the car park. Massive stands. England flags. A giant statue of a line-out – five rugby players leaping for the ball. And there were five words engraved around its base. Teamwork. Respect. Enjoyment. Discipline. Sportsmanship.

All chat had stopped as the bus drove through the streets of outer London. But now there was something more than silence.

It was awe.

That was what Woody was feeling. Jaw-dropping, eye-popping awe. To think that they were going to play here. And not only that – they were playing for the National Schools Trophy. If they won, they would qualify for the next level – the European Schools Trophy. Mr Johnson had told them about that part before, but it hadn't seemed real to Woody until now.

They walked in through the players' entrance past a huge St George's flag and into one of the dressing rooms, where they put their kitbags down on the floor.

Each player had their own place – a piece of card with their name and number above where their shirt was hanging.

On top of Woody's socks and shorts, there was an envelope.

A note from his dad.

Woody. I'm proud of you beyond words.

But words will have to do.

I'm sorry I'm not there with you today.

I'll be watching online.

Love Dad.

SIXTEEN

Walking out through the tunnel at Twickenham was like a dream. The perfect bright pitch. The bounce of the turf beneath their feet. The noise of the crowd, even though there were only 2,000 people in a stadium built for 82,000.

None of it felt real. Woody was struggling to cope with the scale of the stadium and the match he was about to take part in.

Borderlands versus Shadwell. The final of the National Schools Trophy.

On the pitch, Mr Johnson got the players into a huddle before kick-off.

"I want you to focus," he said. "We've worked on this. You are not to think of it as Twickenham until the game is over. This is just a rectangle of grass. A rugby pitch. OK?"

Woody said "OK" like the rest of the boys. But he knew he wasn't focused. There was too much to take in. The size of the stands. The huge blue sky. The sense of history.

And that lack of focus showed once the game kicked off. It was passing Woody by. Passing all the Borderlands team by. They were losing the key plays. They were making mistakes all over the pitch. Giving away points.

And then Woody took a short pass and knocked on. He heard the referee's whistle and David screaming at him at the same time. Right in his face.

"What the hell are you doing?" David yelled. "A knock-on from that? You're a joke."

Scrum to Shadwell.

From the scrum, Shadwell won a penalty. The Shadwell kicker stepped up and scored. 12–0.

The game was slipping away from Borderlands. Fast.

Then it got worse. At the next play, the Shadwell full back took the ball and charged through two Borderlands tackles. In desperation, David dived at the full back, taking him round the neck, both of them spinning to the ground.

After the pushing and shoving between both teams, the referee pulled out a card.

Yellow.

David was sin-binned. Eight minutes to half-time. Down to 14 players.

By the break it was 22–0.

The Twickenham dream was becoming a Twickenham nightmare.

Half-time.

David burst into the dressing room a minute after his team-mates had sat down. Mr Johnson stood at the centre of the room, hands on hips, overseeing a minute of silence before he spoke. He stepped back a little when David came in.

"Can I speak, sir?" David asked.

Mr Johnson hesitated. It was clear he was torn between anger that David had been sin-binned and reduced the team to 14 players, and the fact that his father had just been killed while serving his country. At last, Mr Johnson nodded.

David's face was pink, his eyes red-rimmed, his voice loud and sharp. "That was pathetic," he said. "And I was the worst of us. I'm in the sin bin. Those last ten points? My fault. But you lot – all of you – are letting each other down. And the school down. And Mr Johnson down. What the ..."

David paused. "Can I swear, sir?"

Mr Johnson shook his head.

"What are we doing?" David went on, without drawing breath. "Our heads are in the clouds. Aren't we clever to be playing at Twickenham? No – we're not. I'll be ashamed to tell my family – or anyone else – about this. And you should all be ashamed. Sitting there. You make me sick. I make myself sick ..."

Woody watched David as he ran out of words. Out of anger. He looked close to tears. The days of grief he'd endured were written across his face.

Then Owen stood up. He just stood up and looked at David. No words.

David nodded at Owen.

Next Rory stood up.

Then a couple of the backs: Thomas and Rahim.

Woody followed, standing too.

There was something moving through the room now. Something unspoken. Something that had changed the mood. Woody could feel the hairs prickling on the back of his neck and on his arms.

Now the whole team was standing up and looking at David. Silent. But with him.

David glanced at Mr Johnson.

Mr Johnson smiled. "Lead them out, David."

The second half was going to be different. Woody could tell that as soon as Shadwell School kicked off to restart the game. The mood of the Borderlands players changed everything. David had stirred their passion for the match.

There was now a force to Borderlands' game – an unstoppable force that began to work its magic four minutes into the second half. It was the first scrum after the break. Woody saw that the Borderlands pack were pushing twice as hard, using all their weight. It caught the Shadwell pack by surprise and they turned too fast, leaving three of their players offside.

Penalty.

The first kickable penalty for Rory, who went through his calm routine of focusing his body and his mind before he stepped up.

22–3.

Over the next 30 minutes, Borderlands earned five more penalties. Shadwell School were making more and more errors. They were rattled by Rory. And now they had seen him in action, they knew he was deadly with his foot and any mistake they made could be punished by three points.

And deadly he was. Six from six. The score was 22–18. Five minutes to go.

Shadwell restarted, kicking the ball high at an angle instead of deep into Borderlands territory, trying to keep it in their own possession.

Woody thought it was a mis-kick at first and he wasn't sure what to do. He stooped and picked up the ball. Except he didn't. He fumbled it. And stumbled. And the ball spun away. And Woody heard the whistle.

Knock-on. His second of the game. Scrum to Shadwell well into the Borderlands half.

Woody knew he'd blown it. Borderlands needed possession to have any chance of scoring the five points they needed to win.

Now Shadwell had the ball. Woody could see the grins on the faces of the opposition. They'd been under the kosh – but now they could win it by holding on to the ball.

The clock was running down. Two minutes to go. And then, at last, the ball broke – a fumble from a Shadwell player this time. Nerves on both sides. Woody scrambled for the ball, his first touch since his knock-on.

He bent to take it. He had to get this right. He looked about him. Who to pass to? There was no one. And the Shadwell defenders were almost on top of him.

So Woody dropped the ball onto his foot and kicked it, a grubber kick that spun between three advancing Shadwell players. Then he used every bit of muscle he had to power his body through the defence.

When Woody broke through their line, he caught up with the ball ahead of him and booted it harder, gaining speed all the time. Woody was in his element. He was running. He was in control of a ball. He felt that nothing could stop him.

The Shadwell lines were in disarray.

His third kick came after he had broken through the forwards.

He had clear ground now.

He could hear the Shadwell forwards shouting behind him. But he believed in his pace.

Over the halfway line. 30 metres out. Woody tried to get his boot under the ball for his fourth kick.

The ball bounced, reared up. He had it. 15 metres out.

In the next second, Woody saw two Shadwell players converging on him. And a flash of yellow and blue to his left. A Borderlands shirt.

Jesse. Ten metres wide.

Woody felt the first Shadwell player's hand take his waist. But as he began to go down, he offloaded the ball to his left, spinning it hard.

The ball went straight into the arms of Jesse.

Jesse was eight metres out. He dodged a last desperate Shadwell tackle, then dived for the line.

Try.

Right under the posts.

Woody was aware of some tension in the crowd now. Would Borderlands convert the try? But Woody smiled. He knew that Rory would never miss the kick from there.

A pause. Then Rory stepped up to kick.

And scored.

The game was over. Borderlands had won. They were National Schools Champions.

Woody looked over at the crowd. Some of them were shouting and cheering, others just clapping – all of them on their feet, all of them caught up in the game. And he saw Mr Johnson and Mr Searle dancing on the edge of the pitch.

Then Woody saw David run over to the side of the seating. There was a woman and a girl there. They must be his mum and sister. Woody saw David's sister leap into his arms. The two of them staggered around, half laughing and half crying. There was a sad smile on their mum's face.

Now Woody felt even happier. For David and his family. Their moment of happiness made this win even more of a good thing.

SEVENTEEN

Back in the dorm at Borderlands, Woody flicked on Skype. It was a reflex now. Something he did. Just in case. But – as ever – he knew the chances of his dad being there were one in a thousand.

"Hi, Woody."

Woody nearly fell off his bed. There was his dad's face, close to the camera.

"Dad! Are you OK? What can you tell me?"

"I'm fine, son. Things have calmed down a bit. Let's say I'm getting a bit more time on the ground."

Woody grinned. His dad was safe. That made him feel better than anything. Better than lifting the silver trophy at Twickenham. But he still couldn't wait to tell him about the game.

"I know why you're grinning," his dad said.

"You're OK," Woody said, puzzled. "That's why."

Woody's dad smiled. "I watched a rugby match this afternoon," he said.

"Yeah?"

"Yeah," his dad said. "It was pretty good. There was this centre playing. He was a natural ... er ... footballer."

Woody grinned again, fell back on his bed and began to tell his dad about the match and the news that Borderlands were going to Toulon to play for the European Schools Trophy and that he might be in the team.

"So, what about our deal, Woody?" his dad asked.

"Deal?" Woody asked, although he knew exactly what his dad was talking about.

"About you staying at Borderlands. Until after the war?"

"The deal's still on, Dad."

"Just until I get back?" his dad said. "Then you can choose – football or rugby."

"We'll see, Dad," Woody said. He'd been trying hard not to, but now his face finally cracked into a big smile. A smile that showed he was happy. A smile that showed he couldn't wait to play more rugby.

2

SURFACE TO AIR

ONE

Rory stared in horror from the back seat as the bus he was travelling in veered the wrong way round a roundabout.

He closed his eyes, held on to the seat in front of him and waited for the collision.

A few seconds later, Rory opened his eyes again. Everything was fine. He was an idiot. And he knew it. He was just going to have to accept the fact that he was in France and French people drive on the wrong side of the road.

It wasn't the only new thing to get used to. The billboard ads flashing past were for products Rory couldn't place. And the music on the bus radio was all stuff he'd never heard before.

At home, when Rory and his mum had looked at the town of Toulon on a map, they'd seen that it was by the sea on the south coast of France. So Rory had expected it to be a place of beaches and palm trees. He had not expected warehouses and dual carriageways, traffic jams and beeping horns. Rory couldn't even tell his mum about it. She was thousands of miles away, working for the RAF in the Central Asian Republic. Or somewhere.

To clear his mind of his troubles, Rory scanned the horizon for rugby posts. If he saw rugby posts, he'd be able to imagine kicking the ball over them. And that would help him relax.

Rory's two best friends from school – Owen and Woody – were on the back seat next to him. The three of them were travelling with the rest of the school rugby team to take part in a tournament. Their school – Borderlands – was representing the UK against a team from France, a team from Russia and a team from Italy. They were competing to be European Schools Rugby Champions.

When the bus came off the dual carriageway, Rory looked down at his map. They were heading into the centre of town now. Rory knew that he would get to see rugby posts very soon if they carried on this route, because the bus would head straight past the famous Stade Félix Mayol. It was one of the greatest rugby stadiums in Europe.

"Damn it," Rory heard the boy on the seat in front of him say. That was Jesse. Scrum half, star player and captain of Borderlands rugby team.

"What's up?" another voice asked. That was David, Jesse's friend.

"We're heading right, up into town," Jesse said.

"If we'd gone left here, we'd have seen the harbour. My mum should be here by now. She sailed out of Plymouth ten days ago."

"On your yacht?" David asked.

"Yeah," Jesse said. "The new one. The *Elite*."

Rory looked back at his map and traced the route of the bus with his finger as a way to block out Jesse's voice. Jesse bothered Rory. The idea that his family owned a yacht bothered him too.

When Rory looked back up, he saw it across a tangle of roads. The mighty Stade Félix Mayol. Its stands towered over the road. There was an arch at the corner of the stadium, with the words:

VILLE DE TOULON – STADE MAYOL

On the other side of the arch, there was a hint of green and two sets of posts. Rory yearned to take a ball and start kicking there and then. He half stood up to get a better view. Then he saw Owen smiling at him – his friend knew what he was thinking.

"Do you think they'd let me?" Rory asked.

"I doubt it," Owen said.

"Let him what?" Woody asked.

"Kick," Owen said. "On the pitch."

But Rory wasn't listening to his two friends. He had his eyes closed now. In his mind he was in the stadium and on the pitch. He let the ball fall from his hands, kicked to send a drop goal between those tall white posts.

TWO

Ten of the boys were watching a big TV screen in one of the hotel's meeting rooms when Rory, Owen and Woody joined them. The screen was filled with images of huge planes being loaded with brown boxes and bags of rice, followed by pictures of the same planes taking off down the runway at the RAF base back in England. A commentary in French ran in the background.

Most of the boys were familiar with these scenes. Borderlands was a boarding school and many of its pupils had parents in the RAF. That's why Rory's parents were away. His mum was an engineer who fixed damaged planes and helicopters. His dad supplied ammunition and spare parts to the army.

The boys watched the TV in silence. Most of them didn't understand the French news reader's commentary, but they were glued to the screen anyway. Rory could see that some of the adults were watching it in a worried sort of way too. He spotted David's mum, who had come to help with physio if any of the boys got injured. She was a sports doctor of some sort. David's sister, Taylor, was there as well, and they were both frowning at the screen. But they had every reason to look unhappy – it was only a few weeks since David's dad had been killed when an RAF plane went down over the Central Asian Republic.

"I'm not following this at all. It's too fast. What are they saying?" Rory heard Woody ask Owen.

"The war in the Central Asian Republic is now almost three months old ..." Owen translated from the French. "The British air force is lifting aid into the capital ... the rebels have the capital under siege ... The airlift is the only source of food for the 500,000 civilians trapped there ..."

Rory listened hard to every word to see if the news affected his parents.

"Hang on ..." Owen went on. "Many of the RAF planes have come under ... under fire." He began to look panicked. "The rebels are using ... I think they're saying 'surface-to-air missiles' ... Spaznyit ... something's being supplied by Russia ... the rockets, I think ... the British Prime Minister is in discussions with Russia to bring an urgent stop to this trade ..."

Woody looked at Rory. "I don't believe it," he said. "Do you mean that Russian arms dealers are supplying weapons to the rebels? What the ...?"

The room had filled up – all 20 players were now there to witness Woody's anger. Most of them were nodding in agreement. They all knew that Woody's dad was a Typhoon pilot and that he had good reason to fear surface-to-air missiles.

Then Mr Johnson came in – the head rugby coach

and former Premiership second row was a big man. The boys fell silent as he walked up to the TV. He was joined by his assistant, Mr Searle.

"Please turn this off, boys," Mr Johnson said.

Three boys competed to grab the TV remote.

"Thank you," Mr Johnson said. "Right. We've got training in the morning. But I want to go through a few things. Some house rules. OK?"

When Mr Johnson's team talk had finished and everyone else headed to their rooms, Rory hung back and made for the stairway at the end of the corridor. He had something else to do before he went to bed. As he opened the door, a light flicked on. He walked down to the bottom floor, stretching his thighs and calves as he went. At the bottom, he turned round, checked his watch, took a deep breath, then ran hard up the stairs.

He checked his watch again as soon as he reached the sixth and top floor.

42 seconds.

Then, after a break, he went again.

39 seconds.

Better. But he would beat that by the end of the tournament. He'd get it down to 35. Maybe even 30. That was Rory's challenge to himself.

THREE

The next morning, after breakfast, Rory followed the rest of the Borderlands squad across the hotel lobby and onto a minibus. They were going to the Toulon training ground to prepare for the tournament.

As Rory stood outside in the rising heat, he noticed that the air seemed to smell different here. He could hear French voices coming from an open window. Further up the road a man was hosing the street. Rory watched the rivulets of water snake towards the minibus.

Rory was struck by a clear memory of his dad blasting the moss on the garden path at the house on the airbase where they used to live. He wondered where his parents were. He hated the fact that he didn't know. He liked to look at the map in his diary and put his finger on where they were.

"Come on, boy," Mr Searle called. "On the bus."

The Toulon training ground was amazing. Superb. Nothing out of place.

After a good 15 minutes of warm-up, the Borderlands players ran in attacking formations, two groups of five going at each other. Then the backs were ready for a break. Mr Johnson asked Owen to hand out bottles of water to the others. The backs settled down to watch the forwards practising line-outs. The heat of the sun felt good.

"You're playing well," Rory said to Woody.

"I'm working on it," Woody replied.

Rory smiled. Just a few weeks had passed since Woody had arrived at Borderlands, saying he was into football and nothing else. He was so against the idea of playing rugby that he'd run away from the school on his first night there.

Rory saw Mr Johnson looking over at them and he grabbed his chance.

"Is it OK if I go and get some kicking done, sir?"

Mr Johnson smiled. "Yes, Rory. I'd expect nothing else."

Rory jumped to his feet and walked past the forwards to the posts. He bent to collect a ball from the pitch. "Six from six," he said to himself, then felt for the notebook and pencil in his pocket. He'd record his success – or failure – there, like he always did. He'd also draw the path each kick followed. Then he would be able to look at his notes later and work out exactly where he could improve.

Rory set the rugby ball on the cone, put his right foot just under it, then stared at it.

As he stared, he could hear two of his team-mates talking.

"Did you hear the Russian boys in the hotel reception?" one asked.

It was Jesse. No question.

"No," the other boy said. "What did they say?"

Rory tried to blank out the voices and focus on his kicking. Normally he could do that, but one word Jesse said broke his focus. "Spaznyit." The name for the surface-to-air missiles that the Russians were selling to the rebels.

Rory stood like a statue and listened, his eyes closed so he could have full concentration.

"They were pretending to be planes and making bomb noises," Jesse said. "And they did it right as we walked past."

When the other guy spoke, Rory realised it wasn't another forward at all. It was Mr Searle.

"Did you really hear that?" Mr Searle asked. "Are you sure? We need to do something about it if you did."

"Yes, sir," Jesse replied. "I heard it. They meant it."

Rory took two paces backwards and focused on the ball in front of him again. He could kick this. Even if the conversation was getting to him. Even if the way Mr Searle always agreed with Jesse got to him. Even if there were thoughts of his mum and dad in danger bursting into his mind like shrapnel, he would still kick that ball. It was what he had to do.

One step to the left, and Rory looked up, his eyes on an imaginary dot in the dead centre of the posts. The dot was in his mind first, and then it was burned into the space in the sky.

Rory breathed in.

Mr Searle's voice interrupted his calm again.

"That's a disgrace," he said. "The Russian boys. It's too much. I ..."

Rory moved forwards. Three, two, one – and his foot struck the ball. The ball sailed towards the posts. Then over. Rory stood and stared at it, then heard applause from someone behind him. He saw the ball hit the spot he had burned in the sky.

The clapping might have been Mr Johnson. He had just joined in the discussion about the Russian team. His tone was friendly, but Rory knew that he was giving the assistant coach a telling-off.

"Let's not wind the boys up, shall we, Mr Searle?" Mr Johnson said. "Better we keep our minds on the match, don't you think?"

Rory marked the first kick in his notebook, then he picked up the second ball and walked 20 paces to his left. He wanted a tighter angle for his next kick.

FOUR

At the foot of the stairs, Rory took several deep breaths and listened. There were no sounds from above. That meant he had a clear run without anyone else seeing what he was doing. He warmed up his legs with 12 lunges on each side – left, then right. When his muscles were stretched, he exploded up the stairs.

One breath for each set of ten steps.

That was the plan.

Two sets of ten steps per floor.

Halfway up, Rory knew he had got faster already. He might beat his record.

But at the turn for the second-last floor, Rory

heard a door open. He slowed down so as not to cause a crash.

A woman in a tracksuit top and shorts walked into the stairwell. David's mum. She smiled at Rory – the first smile he'd ever seen from her. He kept going, pumping his arms and legs hard up the last set of steps.

"Hey, Rory," David's mum said. "You never stop, do you?"

Rory smiled, but he was too breathless to speak.

"How long did it take you?" she asked. "Did you beat your record?"

Rory's smile was broader now. This woman knew exactly what he was doing.

"I did," he gasped. He checked his watch. "37 seconds. But my target is 35."

"That's impressive," she said. "I'm doing ten up, ten down. No time limit. No stopping either."

"That's impressive too," Rory said. He remembered David saying that his mum had run marathons. Lots of them. These steps wouldn't be a problem to her.

David's mum nodded, but the smile faded from her face.

Neither of them spoke for a few seconds.

"It takes your mind off things, doesn't it?" she said at last. "It's something to do."

"Yes," Rory said. He didn't know what to say to this woman whose husband had died in an RAF airlift only a few weeks ago. He wanted to make her feel better. But what could he say?

"Do you think about your mum out there?" David's mum asked.

"Sometimes," Rory said.

"She's a fine woman, Rory. David's dad thought the world of her."

Rory rubbed his eyes. Then he looked at David's mum.

"Are you OK?" he asked.

She nodded and smiled again. "Thanks for asking. I'm not too bad most days. It's good to be out here. I'll be on the bench with your coaches tomorrow. It'll be amazing for all you boys to play in a stadium like that, won't it?"

"It will," Rory agreed. And he left David's mum to get on with her steps.

FIVE

It was semi-final day in the Stade Mayol.

The Borderlands boys sat in the main stand, above the halfway line, where they could see the green of the pitch, the city's towering buildings and the sea beyond.

When the two teams came on, cheers and applause echoed round the stadium. Rory estimated that about a thousand people were here to watch the first semi – Scuola Como, from the north of Italy, versus Baskov School from St Petersburg, Russia. Borderlands were playing Castanet of France later.

"They're huge," Woody said, leaning into Rory.

"The Baskov lads, I mean. When you see them next to the Italian lads."

Rory nodded. Woody was right – the Russian boys were massive. He suspected Baskov would use their strength and size and play a hard game.

Less than 30 seconds after kick-off, Rory was proved right. Baskov's game plan was to batter the opposition into submission. Tackles went flying in hard on anyone who had the ball. And the size of the Russian players meant that it looked like men against boys. Scuola Como took huge hits, bouncing off Baskov, hitting the ground hard.

Rory thought that the first scrum was a joke. The Russians overwhelmed the Italians no problem.

By half-time the score was astonishing. Baskov 38 – Como 9.

As the teams trooped off, two Baskov players stared up at the group from Borderlands and scowled at Jesse. Jesse glared back down at the Russian boys.

The rest of the Russian boys stopped and fixed their eyes on Jesse. Mr Johnson had to push Jesse back into his seat before the Russian team would leave the pitch.

"Jesse. Stop it," Mr Johnson said. "Use that anger on the pitch. I don't want to see any nonsense like that from Borderlands boys."

"But they're winding us up on purpose, sir," Jesse spat.

"Yes, they're winding you up," Mr Johnson said. "They want to get a rise out of you. They want to put you off your game later. But they're resorting to mind games because they're scared of us. Understand? Keep yourself under control. Don't make it easier for them."

As Mr Johnson and Jesse argued, Rory climbed out of his seat past Woody and Owen.

"Where are you going?" Owen asked.

"The pitch."

"What? Now?"

"Our game, it's an hour after this one," Rory said. "I need to kick now. There'll be no time later."

"Have you asked Mr Johnson?"

"I need to kick," Rory repeated. He walked down the stand to the metal grilles at the front, where a gate was open.

Rory knew it was a risk going onto the pitch without permission. It was half-time in a semi-final, after all. Of course it felt wrong. It felt like he was breaking a rule. But he had to overcome that feeling, because he needed to kick. Full stop. He knew the others would be looking at him and wondering if he'd lost the plot. Even Mr Johnson. But he didn't care.

Rory took a cone and placed it on the 22-metre line, level with the posts.

All the noise of arguing and the sounds of the city outside the stadium that had been so loud all through the first half faded as Rory began his routine. Six from six. Under pressure. That was what he wanted. He had ten minutes. The time pressure was good too – it would make this harder.

Rory stopped thinking. All that was there was the ball and the posts and the spot that he had burned in the air.

Two steps back. One to the left. Run up. Boot on ball.

His aim was true. Perfect.

*

The first semi-final finished Baskov 72 – Como 24.

It was a crushing defeat. Literally. Baskov School had won the game by being bigger and more brutal than the Italians. They'd given away 13 penalties and lost two players to the sin bin while they were at it. For all that, Rory had to admit that Baskov were devastating when they were running with the ball.

Rory shook his head. "That was ugly," he said. "It'll be tough if we make it to the final."

Owen and Woody agreed.

Then Mr Johnson was leaning in between them. "Minds on our game, lads. You're not in the final yet. The Russian team have been asked to clear the dressing room within 20 minutes, so I'd like to do some warm-ups on the pitch first. Shuttle runs. Stretching. OK?"

"Yes, sir," Rory said. He followed Mr Johnson down the steps and onto the pitch.

Half an hour later, Mr Johnson led his team towards their dressing room. Rory could feel match-day adrenaline rushing through his body. He still found it hard to believe they were about to play in the Toulon stadium.

But when Mr Johnson opened the door to the dressing room they heard loud music. A heavy bass. Boys singing along in rough voices.

Rory was right behind their coach as he entered and he saw 20-plus Russian players. Their kit was all over the floor. Half of them were still in towels.

"Right. Come on, lads," Mr Johnson snapped. He led his team back into the concrete corridor, where he headed towards one of the tournament organisers.

A brief discussion followed.

Rory watched. He hated this. He wanted to be in the dressing room with his head down, thinking about kicking. His nerves were jangling. He didn't need this delay. He needed to go over everything in his mind. He needed things to be like they always were. He needed to know what was going to happen next.

When Mr Johnson returned, Jesse was standing just behind Rory.

"What did they say, sir?" Jesse asked.

"There's been a ... mix-up," Mr Johnson said. "About who is using the dressing room. We'll have to get changed down the corridor. In one of the massage rooms."

Jesse pushed Rory out of the way to move forward.

"There's no mix-up, sir," he said. "They've done it on purpose. They've taken over our dressing room, like they've been taking over the countries around them for the last hundred years."

"Massage room," Mr Johnson repeated.

"Sir, we should get in there and ..."

Mr Johnson stepped towards Jesse. He towered over him. "Team Captain," he barked. "I need you to lead your team to the massage room and keep them calm and focused on the French team we have to play. Not the Russian team who have – as you put it – taken over the dressing room. Got it, Jesse? OK?"

Jesse stepped back, out of the coach's shadow. "Yes, sir," he said in a low voice. Then he turned to the team. "This way, lads."

SIX

For all that Rory thought Jesse was a complete idiot at times, he couldn't do anything but admire him during the next 80 minutes of rugby.

The Borderlands team captain was on fire.

In every play he out-thought and out-skilled the Castanet players. He made the right choice every time. To pass, to offload, to go at the French team. When he passed, he played the right team-mate in. And then he was on hand to take up the ball and storm the French line.

The French team just couldn't handle him.

Jesse's first two tries were under the posts –

that made for easy conversions for Rory. His third try was an amazing double dummy run past three attempted tackles. By then the game was already won. Jesse pushed the last boy out of the way with a flat hand, then touched down on the far right side of the pitch.

Jesse's hat-trick even got the French fans on their feet.

But Rory wasn't thinking about Jesse's wonder-try – he was thinking about his own kick. This one would be harder. Much harder. It was on Rory's weaker foot and as wide as it could possibly be. It was 40 metres to the posts. A tough kick for a grown man, let alone an under-15.

For the team it didn't matter. The score was 30–9, with only a few seconds left. There was no question that Borderlands were in the final of the European Schools Trophy. But it mattered to Rory. He had put over five from five in the Stade Mayol. He wanted six from six. That would look good in his notebook. He couldn't fault himself on that.

Rory moved back two steps and took a deep breath.

Then he took one step to his left. He fixed his eyes between the posts, made his mark in the sky behind them. Breathed out. In. Then he kicked.

Some people in the stands began to applaud.

They thought the ball was over. But Rory knew it wasn't. It came down just short of the crossbar. It wasn't over at all.

After the final whistle, the Castanet players formed a guard of honour and cheered Borderlands off. Rory smiled and nodded as people clapped him on the back. He knew he had to look pleased – that's what would be expected of a team of winners. But then, when everyone was off the pitch, Rory held back, waiting until all the fans had gone and both the teams were in their dressing rooms. Only Jesse was left on the pitch side. He was with a tall woman, who must be his mum – Rory had seen her at rugby matches before – and three men in suits. They were talking in French. But Rory wasn't going to worry about them.

He had something to do.

Rory picked up the match ball and walked to the spot where he'd missed his last kick.

He set the ball up on the cone, breathed in and stepped back two paces.

Breathed out.

In.

A step to the left.

Then he stepped up to the ball and kicked.

Nobody clapped. Nobody cheered. Nobody saw. The ball hit the exact spot Rory had targeted. Just what he had wanted to do earlier.

He felt a little better. But only a little. He wanted to kick all night, try another six from six, but he could see that the floodlights around the pitch were already fading.

Back in the massage room – Borderlands' dressing room for the night – Owen and Woody looked up as Rory came in.

"Well?" Owen asked.

"Well what?" Rory said.

"Did you score?" Owen laughed. "I know why you stayed out there. You had to take that last kick again. So did you score it?"

"I did."

Rory took out his notebook. As he filled it in, Woody stood next to him.

"You missed two announcements," he said.

"Yeah? Who from?"

"Mrs Hampshire."

"What about?"

"Jesse's been offered an under-18 contract with Toulon."

Rory stared at Woody. "Really? That's amazing. Where is he?"

Woody shrugged. "I dunno."

"So what's the other announcement?" Rory asked.

"Oh, yeah ... Jesse's mum is hosting a party for the team."

"Great," Rory said. "It'll be posh. Where?"

"Very posh." Woody nodded. "It's on her yacht. The *Elite*. She's cruising the Med and she's stopped in Toulon harbour for the tournament. She's going to take us all out on the yacht for the party."

"Really?" Rory felt his stomach cramp. He closed his eyes and his thoughts began to rage out of control. He hated boats. Fathoms of water between him and the bottom of the sea. A small space with lots of people and no way off. Anything could go wrong and there'd be nothing he could do.

He would just have to think of a way to get out of the party.

As the other boys filed out of the Stade Mayol, Rory

stayed behind to speak to Mr Johnson, who was checking that the Borderlands dressing room had been left tidy.

"Sir? Please can I be excused from the party on Jesse's boat?" Rory asked.

Mr Johnson looked surprised. "Why, Rory?"

"I can do some extra kicking while you're gone," Rory said. "I need the time."

Mr Johnson looked into Rory's eyes. "You're scared?" he said. "Of water?"

Rory nodded. There was no point in hiding it.

"We all have fears, Rory."

Rory nodded again. "I know," he said. He wondered what Mr Johnson was scared of.

"I want you to come," Mr Johnson said. "But I'll do you a deal. I've an idea for something that might help."

SEVEN

The next day Rory had no choice but to follow the other boys onto the boat for the party. He stuck close to Owen and Woody as they were all greeted by Jesse's mum. She looked elegant in flowing white trousers.

The engine fired and the *Elite* glided out of the harbour. Rory stood with his team-mates and looked in awe at the huge white yachts around them. Each of them had to be worth hundreds of thousands of pounds. Some were as big as buildings. In fact, they were so big that Rory wondered how they could float.

"Look at that," he heard one of the other boys say.

Rory looked and heard himself gasp. Just a few hundred metres away, several French navy ships sat grey and menacing, low in the water. Just beyond the ships, there was an aircraft carrier. It sat there like it was the most normal thing in the world.

Once the *Elite* was out of the bay, Rory and the others went in to eat.

The dining room took up the whole of one floor of the boat. Its glass walls reflected the lights of the city and the port. Rory found it hard to believe it was all real. The boat. The meal. The bay itself.

As Rory stepped inside, he saw that a big TV screen was on and they were serving a buffet. That suited Rory fine. He could grab some food and sit and watch the TV. He wanted fish or chicken – protein to feed his muscles after his last speed and strength workout on the hotel stairs. His record was 36 seconds now.

Rory sat in the only spare seat, next to David, and he and his team-mates watched TV footage of planes taking off in the dark, followed by explosions that filled the screen with yellow and orange light. Rory put down his plate – his appetite was gone.

"What's going on?" he asked David.

"Some sort of attack on Lusa – the capital of the Central Asian Republic," David said. He looked over at his mum. "Mum's had a lot of texts come in. From home. I bet she knows more than the BBC."

Rory looked across the room and studied David's mum's face. Her cheeks were pink. Her eyes were fixed on her smartphone, and one finger was tapping like fury. Taylor sat next to her, frowning at the TV screen.

"Have you asked her?" Rory said.

David looked into Rory's eyes for a moment and then shook his head. "She'll not tell us anything, mate. Whatever she knows she'll tell Mr Johnson, and he'll tell us if he thinks we need to know." He stood up. "But I'll tell you if she tells me, OK?"

Rory nodded. "Thanks."

David walked off and Rory looked over at Owen and Woody. They were both talking to Jesse. Jesse seemed to be shouting, like he was winding Owen up about something. Rory didn't fancy getting involved in that and so he picked up his plate and ate his food, alone. He ate on auto-pilot, not really tasting the food. David's mum smiled at him a couple of times, but she still looked on edge, and she was still reading texts. Rory imagined how hard it must be for her when the armed forces were in action like this. It must remind her of the day her husband was killed.

Rory decided to go out onto the deck. As he got up, a shout came from across the room. Jesse.

"It didn't say that," he yelled.

"It did," Owen shouted back.

Rory stared at the two boys. Their row got even louder.

"I read the subtitles – it didn't say anything about the siege being broken!" Jesse shouted. "I know exactly what's going on. My dad texts me. And he's not told me that the siege is broken. So it isn't. OK?"

Owen looked round at the room. "I just said that the French news reported that the siege was broken," he explained. "They might be wrong. But I'm just telling you what they said."

"How do you know what they said, anyway?" Jesse's voice had changed, and there was a tone of laughter in it now. "You can't even read English, let alone French," he jeered. "Everyone knows you get special lessons."

Rory looked over at Mr Searle, who was standing with Jesse's mum. He was the only teacher in the room. He seemed to be smiling, like he thought it was OK for Jesse to say those things to Owen. Rory couldn't believe it. He should be stepping in. Now. No wonder none of the boys liked him.

"I heard what the reporter said," Owen said. "I can speak French ..." But his voice tailed off, like he'd run out of energy.

All the other voices in the room went silent. Mr Johnson was standing in the doorway. His eyes could have bored holes in granite.

"Jesse," Mr Johnson growled. "Outside. Now. And, Mrs Hampshire – please can you join us?"

Rory slipped past Mr Johnson and out onto the deck. He didn't want to witness whatever was going to happen next. He walked round to the back of the boat. He knew there would be nobody there. Everyone was in the TV room, gripped first by the war and now by Jesse's bad behaviour.

Across the water, Toulon looked amazing. The

lights of the waterfront bars and streets were reflected on the water. The angular shapes of the French fleet were ghostly shadows in the gloom. The lights of the buildings dotted over the mountainside were like little stars suspended in the sky.

Rory took this time alone to think about his parents. He wondered if they were in Cyprus, where RAF personnel often ended up. If they were, they were only a few hundred miles across the sea from here. Rory looked out into the huge black void of sea and night sky. That way. South-east of here.

Then voices interrupted his thoughts.

"Let's talk here, Jesse, Mrs Hampshire," Mr Johnson said. "It's a bit more private."

Rory wondered if he should let Mr Johnson know that he was there. But it was too late. Too embarrassing. So he decided to stay still, then leave as soon as he could, before they saw him.

"I want to talk to you about what went on in there, Jesse," Mr Johnson said. "And I want your mum to be present."

"Yes, sir."

"I don't understand what the fuss is about, Mr Johnson," Jesse's mum interrupted, in the party voice she had been using since they all came on board the yacht.

Rory heard Mr Johnson breathe in like he always did when he was cross. "I just witnessed Jesse being very personal with one of the other boys, Mrs Hampshire. What Jesse said to Owen was out of order."

"He was just teasing," Mrs Hampshire said. Her voice was still light and cheerful.

"I'm afraid it was closer to bullying than teasing, Mrs Hampshire," Mr Johnson came back. "And I am sorry to say this, as we are guests on your yacht.

But I must discipline the boys. Jesse, this is your last chance. We've had this talk more than once. Another episode like this and I will find another captain and consider removing you from the team."

"Well, I don't see why ..." Mrs Hampshire's voice had changed. It was less playful now.

"I am responsible for all the boys," Mr Johnson said. "I could wait until we're not on your yacht, Mrs Hampshire. Or we can deal with this now."

Jesse broke in. "Mr Johnson's right, Mum. I'm sorry, sir. I was wrong to say what I said. I'll apologise to Owen as soon as I can."

"No. You shouldn't have to apologise ..." Mrs Hampshire's voice tailed off.

"But I will," Jesse said. "I'll apologise." Rory heard a note of desperation in his voice.

"Good," Mr Johnson said. "Mrs Hampshire?"

Rory knew why Jesse was ready to apologise.

He'd had his warning. And when Mr Johnson gave a warning like that, he meant it.

Just then, a waft of engine smoke caught in Rory's nose. He sneezed. The conversation stopped.

Rory didn't dare move. Or breathe. Was he about to be discovered? That would not be good at all.

There was a long pause. They were listening. Rory knew that.

"Mrs Hampshire," Mr Johnson said. "I'm sorry I've had to speak to your son like this when I am your guest. But he has responded well and made a good choice."

"That's no problem at all, Mr Johnson," Jesse's mum said, in her cheerful party voice again. "Shall we leave the boys to sort this out? You can join me on the bridge. You said earlier you'd like to have a go at steering the *Elite*."

EIGHT

Breakfast the next morning was quiet. The day before, they'd won a European semi-final – they should be buzzing. But there was a lot else happening. The war on TV. The Russian boys winding Jesse up. Jesse winding Owen up. Being away from Borderlands. There were plenty of reasons for the boys to feel uneasy. And Rory knew that one of the main reasons was the party the night before. Some people had had a great time on the *Elite*. Others hadn't.

Mr Johnson stood up once everyone was sitting and eating. "Listen up, boys," he said. "We need to clear our heads. You agree?"

No one replied.

Mr Johnson went on regardless. "So, this morning," he said, "we're not training. We're going for a walk."

There were a couple of moans. A groan.

"Where?" a back called Thomas asked.

"You've seen that mountain behind Toulon?" Mr Johnson said. "Mont Faron."

They all nodded and mumbled, "Yes."

"We're going up that," Mr Johnson said. "At the top, there's a cafe. Whoever makes it to the top can have a large steak and a drink on me. OK?"

It was a long, tough walk, taking over two hours. The mountain was steep and dry and rocky, with a path that dog-legged left and right all the way up.

At the start, some of the lads complained, but as

they walked up the rough track chat and laughter broke out.

It was warm, but not too hot, and the views were amazing. Sunlight glinted off the French fleet in the water below.

At last, Rory could see that Toulon was a beautiful place. Yes, there were dual carriageways, but there were also woods and beaches and that spectacular harbour.

By the time they reached the top, Rory was buzzing.

"This is working," he said to Owen and Woody. "Loads of people are chatting. Relaxing."

"But we still need to do something about Jesse," Owen said. "Some of the other lads are blanking him. After ... you know ..."

"He deserves it," Rory said. "After what he said to you."

"Maybe," Owen said. "But that's not going to win us the final tomorrow, is it?"

The team was sitting in a cafe on the edge of a mountain top.

There were white tablecloths, bottles of water and silver cutlery catching the sun. A sheer drop fell away below the tables where they sat. They could see for miles across the sea.

Rory was pleased to be sitting opposite David's mum and sister.

"Have you broken 35 seconds yet, Rory?" David's mum asked.

"Not yet." Rory smiled, pleased she had remembered. "But I will."

"I don't doubt it," she said.

But when the steaks were finished, an

uncomfortable silence settled back over the Borderlands players.

Rory watched Mr Johnson talking to Mr Searle. He could tell from their faces that they knew the team spirit had been broken – and Mr Johnson's idea for a walk had not fixed it.

But then Owen jumped to his feet. He raised his voice. "Can I say something, sir?"

Mr Johnson nodded. "Yes, Owen," he said.

Rory watched Owen take a couple of deep breaths.

"We've got a problem, Jesse," Owen said. He turned to face the team captain.

Jesse leaned back in his seat and folded his arms. "Yeah? What's that?"

Rory wondered if Owen's gamble was going to backfire. Jesse was already on the defensive.

"The problem is that we're going to lose the final tomorrow," Owen went on.

Jesse said nothing.

"We're going to lose because we've lost our team spirit," Owen said. "And that's Jesse's and my fault."

"Not yours," Thomas said.

"I don't know." Owen smiled. "But if we don't sort this, then we'll lose. You're right that Jesse wasn't at his best on the boat yesterday."

Everyone's eyes were on Jesse now. How was he going to react to that?

Owen didn't give their captain a chance to speak. "But that's Jesse," he went on. "One minute he's like that, the next he's winning us game after game. We need him. Without him, we're very good. With him, we're the best. So we have to decide. Do we want to take the European Schools Trophy home on the flight in two days? Or do we want it to go to Russia?"

Rory saw the change in the team right away. Some of the boys were sitting up, their backs straight. They'd put their glasses down. Rory felt it inside himself too. Something powerful.

Owen turned to Jesse. "Do you want to win the trophy?" he asked.

"Course I do," Jesse said.

Owen pushed his chair back and walked over so he was face to face with Jesse. Rory saw Mr Johnson lean forward, ready to stand, in case a fight broke out.

"Two more questions?" Owen said.

"If you like."

Rory watched Jesse's hands as he bunched them into fists.

"Are we going to win this trophy if you're in the team?"

Jesse didn't hesitate. "Yeah."

"And are you sometimes an idiot – an idiot who annoys the rest of the team?"

Now Jesse did hesitate. He stalled for time with a cough, clearing his throat.

Rory stared down the mountain. It was so steep. If you slipped and fell, you'd drop for ages before you hit the rocks and trees at the bottom.

At last Jesse spoke. "I suppose."

Rory noticed Mr Johnson ease back in his chair.

Owen stuck his hand out. "OK then, mate," he told Jesse. "I want to see you lift that trophy tomorrow. I want to see you in front of assembly with it back at school. I want to see pictures of you in *Rugby World*, holding the European Schools Trophy in your idiot hands."

There was a pause. Everyone was looking from Owen to Jesse, then back again.

"So do I," Jesse said, putting his hand out too.

NINE

The squad went down Mont Faron in the cable car, in order to save their legs. And Mr Johnson kept his promise to Rory. Back at the hotel, he came to the boys' room. They were watching news footage of the war.

"Rory," said Mr Johnson. "I said if you came to the party on the boat I'd let you kick. And you did. You've got two hours. Go and kick. I've sorted it with Toulon."

Rory grabbed his kit and ran to the Toulon training ground. He was over the moon to get away from the TV. Running like this, then kicking, would help a lot.

When Rory arrived at the training ground, he saw a man kicking at the far end. There was a bag of six balls and a cone waiting for Rory.

He walked out onto the main pitch, set his first ball at the near end and took out his notebook. He wrote down the date.

Six from six.

If he focused on six from six, he wouldn't need to think about anything else.

Rory glanced at the man kicking at the other goal. He felt like he'd seen him before. Was he a rugby player Rory had seen on TV during the Six Nations?

Rory shook himself. This was no time for star-spotting. He had work to do.

Kick one was level with the posts. It went over perfectly.

Kick two was from ten metres left of the posts. It was perfect too.

But when he came to kick three, Rory hit trouble. Big trouble.

Four lads came walking across the pitch out from the trees. They looked like they were making for Rory.

Rory lined up his kick and emptied his mind, trying to ignore the lads as they approached. He assumed they'd walk past, so he could kick. Just kick. That was all he wanted to do, no matter who the lads were.

But they didn't walk past him.

They stopped. They stood there and blocked the ball's flight to the posts.

Now that Rory could see them up close, he knew who they were. They were Russian players from Baskov.

Rory felt his heart rate pick up, but he focused on the ball again.

Then one of the Russians spoke.

"Spaznyit."

And something went in Rory's mind. He couldn't see the ball any more. In fact, he could see nothing but the boy who had spoken. His face. His insolent grin.

Rory went at him, two hands to the chest, hitting him with such force that the boy fell, tumbling backwards on himself. One of the other Russian lads dropped on his knees beside him. Then the other two came at Rory. The first punch hit his cheek hard, and Rory felt his knees go. Another blow, to the gut, and Rory was down. Vulnerable.

Rory brought his knees into his chest just before the first kick landed. He felt a hot shaft of pain shoot from his neck, down his legs, then back again.

TEN

Rory curled into a ball as he felt the sharp pain of a kick on his back. Another jolted through his kidney.

Then he heard the shouting. At first, he thought it was some abuse the Russians were throwing at him to go with the kicking. But then he realised that the words were in French.

The kicking stopped.

Rory fell on his back and opened his eyes. He was dazzled by the floodlights and didn't see the man bending over him until he felt a hand on his shoulder.

"*Tu es OK?*"

The touch was gentle. Not an attacker.

"*Oui*," Rory said, clearing his throat. He hoped it was true. "Er ... *merci*."

The man helped Rory to sit up.

"English?" the man asked.

"Yes ... I mean, *oui*."

The man laughed. "You must be careful getting up. You are perhaps injured."

"I don't think it's bad," Rory said. "I feel OK." But he took his time to stand up. He didn't want to aggravate anything that might keep him out of the final. His back felt bruised, but nothing deep. No muscle damage.

"Where did they go?" Rory asked.

"They run when I shout," the man said. "Cowards. You know them?"

Rory shook his head. "Thank you for helping me," he said. "I'm Rory. From Borderlands School. We're training here."

"I am Jean," the man said. "Jean Valjean. I am from the Rugby Club Toulon."

"What?" Rory stepped back so that he wasn't staring at the man against a floodlight, and he took a good look at him. It was Jean Valjean. *The* Jean Valjean. European Cup winner. Shorter than your average rugby player. Lean but muscular. The French fly half.

"I've seen you," Rory said, star-struck despite himself. "You were playing for Toulon in the Heineken Cup. And for France. At Twickenham."

"Yes," Valjean said. "And I have seen you. Playing for Borderlands. In Stade Mayol. You score five from six. It is good?"

"No," Rory said in a low voice. "Not as good as six from six."

Valjean laughed. "You will never be happy, no?"

Rory smiled.

Valjean squatted to pick up the ball Rory had been about to kick. "Perhaps we train together now? I have watched you. You kick perfect. But one thing. You need to ... how you say ... kick through ...?"

"Follow through?" Rory asked.

"Yes. Follow through. Good. I show you?"

"Yes please," Rory said.

When Rory returned to the hotel, he was buzzing, desperate to tell someone what had just happened. But when he got back to their floor, he saw that all his team-mates were in their common room watching the TV again. And Rory's news was nothing compared to what the TV news had to say. Owen was standing next to the screen, translating.

"The RAF has scored a victory ..." Owen said. "Erm ... after 48 hours of bombing ... the enemy ...

er, rebels have retreated to positions in the mountains … the siege of Lusa is …"

Owen steadied himself on a chair. He grinned.

"It's over. They say … it's a victory for the RAF. For now …"

A massive cheer went up. Rory grinned and turned to Woody. Woody grabbed him and hugged him. He looked around and saw other boys and the adults hugging too. He wanted to cry. But he wouldn't. Not here. Not now.

Later. Only later would Rory let himself cry.

Because now he knew his parents were safe.

ELEVEN

Mr Johnson sent the boys to bed early that night. Rory understood why. For one thing, it was the night before the final and they needed the rest. But Mr Johnson also didn't want the Borderlands players walking the corridors of the hotel where they could bump into Russian players. He wanted to be safe rather than sorry.

Rory had intended to tell Mr Johnson about the attack at the training ground, but he couldn't get his coach on his own and it wasn't something he wanted to share with anyone else. It was serious, but Rory reckoned it would be better for Borderlands if no one else knew about it. Not before the final, anyway. So he kept it to himself. And because he didn't say anything about the attack, he didn't say anything about meeting Valjean either.

When Rory got into bed, he sat and looked at his notebook. He read his kicking results over the last three games he'd played in. The number of kicks he had scored and missed. He fixed on the numbers, not the feelings. Diagrams of angles and distances. It helped calm him. Rory had sensed a build-up of nerves earlier that evening in the team talk and he needed to stop it interfering with his sleep.

Owen was in the bed next to him, already asleep. His breath was slow and steady as if he had nothing to worry about at all. Rory knew he should be asleep by now too, so he reached for the light switch.

Just then, a violent crash came from the room above.

Owen sat up instantly. "Mum? What did you do that for?"

Rory smiled to himself, struggling to suppress a laugh. Woody pulled the bedcovers over his head.

There was another crash. A layer of dust dropped from the ceiling.

Then there were voices in the corridor.

Owen woke up properly. "Who's that?" he asked.

"Jesse."

Rory stood up and opened the door. Owen was right behind him.

Jesse was in the corridor, ranting. "It's the Russian team, sir," he shouted. "They're banging on the floor in every room. They're trying to keep us awake. They're trying to get to us. I reckon we go up there, sir. They want to wind us up before the game."

"And it's working, Jesse, isn't it?" Mr Johnson sighed. "Calm down and listen to me."

The boys gathered in the corridor, facing their coach, as if it was the most normal thing in the world to have a team talk at midnight in their pyjamas.

Mr Johnson shook his head, then smiled.

"Boys. We are not going to win tomorrow by being negative," he said. "We must do it by being positive. Let the Baskov lads play their stupid games. Let them exhaust themselves. We have to let it go. We have to sleep. We have to dream and remember that we are here to play rugby."

In the end, Mr Johnson agreed to go up to the Russian team's floor. The banging stopped a few minutes later.

By then Rory was in bed, lights out. But he could feel the unwanted adrenaline in his system now. The

Russian team's plan had worked on Jesse and it had worked on Rory too.

But Rory had a way to calm himself down. It was based on something he had learned to do to help him control his mind when he thought he might be losing it.

Rory imagined that he was at the foot of Mont Faron in his running gear. He drew a picture in his mind of the path that weaved left then right, up to the cafe where the team had eaten steak earlier in the day.

Then Rory began to run up the path, in his mind. The cable car whirred over him and the hot air cooled as he climbed higher and higher. He imagined the crumbling stone path, the French navy fleet in the distance, the sun rising. Warmth on his skin as he ran at a steady pace up the hill.

Rory was asleep in minutes.

TWELVE

The Stade Félix Mayol. Toulon. Home of one of the finest – and richest – teams in European rugby. Four huge stands. A perfect rectangle of pitch. And a deep blue French sky.

It was the first scrum in the final of the European Schools Trophy.

As soon as Jesse took the ball from the feet of Danny, the Borderlands number 8, two huge Russian boys targeted him. They hit him hard. Flattened him.

Penalty to Borderlands, deep in their own half.

Rory kicked the ball into touch, just over the halfway line, and gained them 30 metres.

The line-out that followed became a maul, then the referee called for a scrum.

And it happened again. The Russian boys smashed Jesse the moment his hands were on the ball.

A Baskov player was warned.

Another penalty. 35 metres out.

Rory understood the Russian game plan. They knew that Jesse was the Borderlands playmaker and they would batter him. They'd give away penalties all day – as long as they thought the kicks were out of Rory's range. And as long as they thought they could put Jesse out of action.

Jesse shook his head and picked up the ball.

"I'll kick it," Rory said.

"Too far," Jesse said. "You'll miss."

"They'll smash you all day if we don't start punishing them for it, Jesse."

Rory watched as Jesse thought.

"Can you do it?" Jesse asked at last.

"Yes," Rory said.

And he could. He would. There was no other thought in his head – and no point in thinking anything else. The ball had to go on the cone, off his boot and between the posts. He'd already seen it happen in his mind. No matter that it was beyond the usual range of an under-15 player. He could do it.

Rory heard some of the Baskov players laughing when he set the ball down on the cone. He ignored them. They could goad him all they liked. They wouldn't get to him. Not while he was on the field of play.

Rory flexed his leg muscles. "I can do this," he told himself. "My legs are stronger now. I've got better technique." The stair runs had helped. As had the follow-through tips from Jean Valjean. They'd give his kicks an extra ten metres, if he believed in himself. And he did believe.

Rory stepped back two paces, then one to the side. He breathed in, then out. Closed his eyes, then opened them. He was alone on the pitch. Just him, the ball, the posts. Then he stepped up, kicked and followed through – forcing his leg right through the kick.

An echo of his boot striking the ball came back off one of the buildings around the stadium. It sounded bizarre. But Rory knew that the ball was over the moment he hit it.

He closed his eyes again, felt a hand on his shoulder. Then Woody's voice said, "Fantastic, Rory."

And Rory knew he'd done something special. He'd found those extra metres on his kicking. Maybe an extra ten. Now he could really get at the Russian team.

The rest of the first half was tough.

Baskov didn't let up their aggressive game. They

had a player sin-binned after 11 minutes, then another after 27. But Borderlands still struggled to make ground. Rory could see that his team-mates were rattled. Their normal fluent passing was absent. They made mistakes, especially in their own half.

By half-time Borderlands had given away nine penalties. The Baskov fly half had scored three of them.

And despite all the foul play, the Russians had given away only three kickable penalties.

Rory had slotted away all three.

9–9. Half-time.

Rory watched the Baskov players jog off the pitch as soon as their captain had kicked the ball into touch. They seemed to have a lot of energy left. Then Rory watched his own team-mates. Their heads were down, their legs heavy – they looked tired. Some seemed to be carrying minor injuries. It had been a battle – a war. And it was clear which team felt it was winning.

THIRTEEN

The second half was the hardest 40 minutes of rugby Rory had ever played. He could feel it in his muscles. He felt weak when he tried to run with the ball and pass it. He had never felt like this before in a game of rugby. His body was spent. And his mind wasn't far behind it.

He could see that the same was true of his team-mates. And of the Russian team too.

Everything was slower. Harder work. More careless mistakes. As a result, there were more penalties – seven more. Rory had kicked his two. The Russian fly half had scored one of his five.

It was 15–12 to Borderlands with minutes to go.

It was hard to believe Borderlands were that close to winning. But Rory knew he had to focus on each play, not on the final score. And not on the trophy.

Rory had been watching the Baskov fly half. He could see that his legs were going. He was refusing kicks over 25 metres now.

Another scrum.

Borderlands had the feed.

Rory heard Jesse shouting, "Possession. Keep possession." Then he tapped the ball on one of the prop's shoulders and fed the scrum.

But the scrum bit back. The Baskov pack had more in their legs after all. And the Borderlands pack was struggling. Rory watched Jesse panic and join the flanker in the maul for the ball along with Rahim and George.

Rory stepped back. They were strung out now. If the Russians got the ball away cleanly …

He broke off this thought before it finished. The Russian scrum half was firing a fast ball ten metres across to his line of backs.

Baskov had six men on Borderlands' four.

One more pass and it was four on two.

Rory ran as hard as he could to grab at the boy with the ball. His arms slipped down the player's knees, then his calves. Rory felt the Baskov winger's boot catch his face. He'd missed the tackle.

The roar of the Russian players – and the shouts from the crowd – told Rory all he needed to know.

Try.

The unthinkable.

17–15 to Baskov. And a kick to come.

As the Russian fly half lined up the kick, Rory stood up and ran over to Jesse. He had to let his captain know that the Russian kicker was losing range.

"Jesse?" he shouted.

But Jesse wasn't listening. He was staring at the blocks of flats that crowded the sky north of the Stade Mayol.

"Jesse!"

"What?" Jesse's voice was angry. It was the tone of a defeated captain, no question.

Rory watched David go up to Jesse and push him to bring him to.

"Listen!" David shouted. "It's critical. Listen to Rory."

At last, Rory had his captain's attention. Only David could have done that.

"He'll miss the kick," Rory said. "He's lost his range. He'll kick it too short. Then we'll restart quickly."

The boys went quiet as they watched the Baskov fly half set up the kick. Jesse lined the backs up as Rory had told him. Now they watched the fly half run up hard and strike the ball.

"Too short," Rory said again. And Rory was right. The fly half hit the ball high but not long enough. It dropped ten metres before the posts. Rory stooped to collect the ball for the restart.

But he knew that, with just two minutes on the clock, Borderlands had to play it fast. The British players took their positions swiftly. Rory kicked off from the halfway line, choosing to aim it hard and low, intending to force an error from one of the Russians.

And it worked. A Baskov player ran forwards to gather the ball, but because it was coming at him at speed, he fumbled it, knocking on.

A scrum to Borderlands. There was hope.

Rory stood back, breathing deeply. He wanted as much oxygen as possible – in his lungs, in his muscles, in his blood.

This was it. The moment of truth.

Rory watched Jesse urge the pack on. Shout at them. They had to win this scrum. Then Jesse had to get the ball back to Rory.

Another deep breath. Rory needed the power in his legs.

The scrum went down. Rory heard the two packs slap against each other. He watched the legs of the two props, their thighs pushing on, their studs ripping up the famous pitch of the Stade Mayol.

Then he saw the ball, a fleck of white moving through the forest of legs.

Into Jesse's hands.

FOURTEEN

Rory watched Jesse as his hands hovered over the ball at the back of the scrum. Then Jesse looked over his shoulder. Right into Rory's eyes.

Rory mouthed, "Yes."

Jesse's hands were on the ball now. He was looking down. Then he twisted his body, his arms going forward. A flick of his wrists and the ball was coming at Rory.

It was spinning. Light coming off it.

Rory changed the position of his feet. He felt the ball in his hands.

He looked up. Five Russian players were coming at

him. He knew two of them. They were his attackers from the night before.

But they were too late. They might get Rory, but they wouldn't get the ball.

The ball fell from Rory's hands.

It hit the ground as he swung his foot.

Contact.

Rory made sure that he followed through. Just like Jean Valjean had shown him. He gave it everything. Then he fell, just as two of the Baskov players hit him.

But Rory felt no pain. He didn't care about them – he knew the ball was up and away. And he knew that it was over.

Three points for the drop goal.

Borderlands 18. Baskov 17.

There was a scuffle above Rory as he lay on the ground.

Then the whistle. It was over.

Borderlands were the champions of Europe.

Rory felt arms around him, then his legs go, bodies on top of him. There were shouts. Cheers. Slaps on Rory's back, his shoulders, his head. He felt drained. He wasn't sure he'd be able to pick up a ball now, let alone kick one.

But as he lay there, Rory felt OK. He couldn't move, but he was OK. Like he was finally satisfied.

And the thing that made him feel the most OK – the thing that was buzzing through his body – was that he had six from six. Five penalty attempts and a drop goal. All of them over the posts.

He hoped Jean Valjean was in the stadium to see it.

Rory stood next to Owen and Woody as they watched their team captain step up to collect the European Schools Rugby Trophy.

The players from the three other teams stood on either side of the small stage, but Jesse didn't look at them as he approached. He stepped up onto the stage and took the trophy in both hands, then turned and lifted it.

A huge cheer echoed through the Stade Mayol. Most of the other players were cheering and clapping. And there were still several hundred people in the main stand. Rory spotted Jesse's mum, and David's mum and sister. All of them waving and grinning.

When Jesse brought the trophy over to the rest of the team, he walked just a fraction too close to the Russian players. Rory saw how he glared into each of the Baskov players' eyes, saying nothing. The Russian boys looked furious, but none of them reacted.

Rory shook his head. Jesse just couldn't help

himself. He couldn't let things lie. Maybe that was what made him such a brilliant player.

Woody interrupted Rory's thoughts. "We're European champions. I can't believe it," he said. "Do you reckon we're going to get a medal?"

Owen shoved Woody with his shoulder. "Not all of us. But there is a Player of the Tournament award."

"Jesse might as well have stayed on the stage then," Rory said.

Owen and Woody laughed.

"Can you believe we're in the World finals now?" Woody said. "New Zealand. Amazing."

Rory shuddered at the thought of 28 hours of travel on a plane. He didn't fancy that at all. But he knew he wasn't supposed to worry about the future. He was meant to enjoy the moment today.

Then he saw Jean Valjean.

The French international stood on stage next to

the official who'd given Jesse the trophy. So Jesse was going to receive his Player of the Tournament award from Valjean. Wow! Rory hoped Jesse would recognise him.

"And now it is time to award the Player of the Tournament medal," the official announced.

Rory watched Jesse hand the trophy to David.

"Jean Valjean has kindly agreed to award it," the official went on.

There was a cheer from the crowd. Valjean was one of their big heroes.

"The winner of the Player of the Tournament medal is ..." Jean Valjean hesitated as he read the piece of paper he'd been handed, then a smile broke out across his face. He looked at Rory. "Is ... Rory Samsudin!"

Rory stared at Jean Valjean. Had he heard him right?

"Yes, you," Valjean said into his microphone. "You kick six from six. It is perfect, no?"

So Rory walked up to collect his award. He took Valjean's hand and shook it.

"Thank you," he said.

"No problem." Jean Valjean grinned. "Congratulations."

Then Rory turned round to face his team-mates. He raised the award – not above his head, just a slight raise to say thank you to his team-mates, who were all clapping and smiling.

Even Jesse was clapping. In fact, Jesse's grin was the biggest of all. He was the captain who had led his team to the World Schools Trophy finals in New Zealand. He was the star player, who'd been talent-spotted for a contract with Toulon. And he was a good enough captain to know he couldn't have done it without Rory.

As he held the award, Rory knew that all his training had paid off. Right at the end, he'd kept his head and put Jean Valjean's expert tips into practice – and kicked the six from six he so desperately wanted to kick.

But now the game was over, Rory wanted the pitch to clear. He wanted the fans to leave. The officials. The Baskov players. Even the Borderlands lot. He wanted to be alone on this perfect green pitch. Just him and a bag of six balls. He wanted six from six. Again.

Rory knew that this was only the beginning.

3

DEADLOCKED

ONE

When the plane had taken off from Heathrow and the seatbelt signs had gone off, Miss Evans leaned across and handed Owen a book.

"What's this, miss?" Owen said. He knew the question sounded daft as he asked it.

"A book," Miss Evans said. "For you."

Owen turned it over in his hands and smiled. A present from Miss Evans. That was kind. Really kind. But it was a book.

Deep down inside, Owen had that feeling he always had when books were involved. The churning worry that he wouldn't be able to finish it. But he wouldn't give in to that this time. Miss Evans had given him this, and he could see that it wasn't just any book. It was called *Calon* and the cover was a red Welsh rugby shirt. If there was any book in the world he wanted to read, then this was it.

"Thank you, miss," Owen said as the plane dipped to the left and they headed over the clouds towards the Equator and on to New Zealand.

Owen wasn't the only 15-year-old boy on the flight. There was a whole bunch of them, including his two best mates from Borderlands – Woody on his left and Rory on his right. All three were members of the school rugby team, and they were heading to Auckland to take part in the four-team World Schools Rugby Trophy. Owen couldn't believe it was really happening.

One of the main reasons they were here was sitting in the seat in front of them. Jesse. The team captain. Their star player. Jesse had just signed an under-16 contract with Toulon in France. He was exceptional on the pitch. But he was also an idiot off it. Not someone to get on the wrong side of.

"Tell me again, how many hours will this flight take?" Rory asked Owen.

"Twenty-six altogether," Owen said.

"That's a loooong time," Woody muttered as he tapped at the video screen on the back of the seat in front of him. He found the BBC News pages and Rory and Owen leaned forward to look.

FIRST FORCES COMING HOME
RAF heads back to UK after conflict in
Central Asian Republic

Owen smiled. That was good news for most of his team-mates on this flight. Borderlands was no ordinary school – at least half the pupils had parents in the RAF who'd been involved with the conflict. The RAF had defended the capital city of Lusa and helped its terrified and starving people. One boy who was on the flight – David – had lost his father when a transporter plane was shot down as it delivered aid.

But now the RAF were coming home.

"I'm pleased for you," Owen said to Rory and Woody. "Really pleased."

"Thanks." Rory smiled.

"Yeah, thanks." Woody nodded.

Owen was surprised that his friends didn't sound happier at the news. They were still staring at the screen.

"I thought you'd be happy," Owen said. "Now it's over."

"It's not that easy," Rory admitted, and then he fell silent again.

Then Woody chipped in. "When I know my dad's

coming back soon, I feel sort of worse than when he's out there," he said. "It's so close. But stuff could still happen ..."

Owen looked at his two friends, trying to understand.

Rory went on. "But the fact they're coming home when we're going away makes it worse too. I seriously thought about not coming so I could see Mum and Dad home safe."

Owen nodded like he understood. But he didn't, not really. He would never understand what it was like to have a parent in the RAF. He couldn't. Imagine knowing your dad was in a plane and someone was firing surface-to-air missiles at him.

Somewhere over Turkey, Jesse spotted Owen's book.

Owen had been reading it in short bursts so

he could keep focused. But it was late now, after midnight back in the UK. He was sleepy.

"How many pages have you read?" Jesse asked.

"What?" Owen said.

"How. Many. Pages. Have. You. Read?"

Owen knew that this was not a normal friendly question. Jesse didn't do normal friendly questions. He was bored and looking for ways to amuse himself. Maybe he hoped other people were listening so he could show off.

"I'm not sure," Owen said. He stared hard at Jesse.

"Not sure?" Jesse smiled.

"That's right, Jesse."

"Does that mean you can't count – *and* you can't read?" Jesse mocked. "Bad luck, mate." He held up a super-thin, top-of-the-range Kindle. "Have you got one of these?"

"No," Owen muttered.

"Get with the programme," Jesse sneered. "I've got loads of books on this. I bet I could read them all before you've struggled to the end of chapter 1 of that one."

"Good for you, Jesse." Owen turned away from Jesse and saw that Mr Johnson, head rugby coach at Borderlands, was studying the two of them. Mr Johnson had a look on his face that said "stop what you're doing". And he was aiming that look at Jesse.

Jesse went back to his Kindle.

"You OK, Owen?" Mr Johnson asked.

"Yes, sir."

"Good. Try and get some sleep, son."

TWO

"This is awesome," Owen said as he gazed across the First XV pitch at Auckland Grammar School. "No wonder they're so good at rugby in New Zealand."

Woody and Rory grinned in agreement.

The Borderlands team were on the other side of the world – 12,000 miles from home. Owen felt exhausted and excited at the same time. He was buzzing and completely whacked, just like everyone else. But they had all agreed to stay awake until it was night in New Zealand. And so Auckland School's Head of Sports was showing them around. Players from the host school had joined them too. The different teams hadn't spoken to each other yet, but they'd swapped a few friendly smiles.

The tour took them to the gym, the main hall and three perfect rugby pitches. Before that, wood-panelled corridors lined with trophies and photos of Auckland Grammar School players since 1869. Serious, determined faces of boys from over a hundred years ago. And a roll of honour – a list of the 51 boys who'd gone on to play for the All Blacks. No school in New Zealand had sent more players to the team.

What a history! This was some school.

Owen watched Rory kneel and touch the grass, then stare hard at the rugby posts at the end of the pitch.

"This is a perfect surface," Rory said. "Give me a ball. I need to kick one. Now."

Owen and Woody laughed. They'd only been in

the country a few hours and already Rory wanted to kick a perfect six from six.

"As long as they don't start doing the Haka," Jesse interrupted in a loud voice.

"Will they?" Owen asked, excited. "That would be great. Imagine that before a match. It'd be awesome."

"Don't be an idiot," Jesse said, and his lip curled. "It wouldn't be fair. It's cheating. Everyone knows that."

Owen noticed two of the Auckland boys look over and he felt a hot surge of anger with Jesse. How could anyone say that the Haka was cheating? How embarrassing was that?

Owen also noticed that Mr Johnson was watching. Owen thought that the rugby coach was watching how he reacted to what Jesse had said. It was as if he wanted Owen to sort the argument out. Mr Johnson was like that – he'd give the boys every chance to do the right thing on and off the pitch.

Owen knew what he had to do. He couldn't let the Auckland boys think that all the Borderlands team were as ignorant as their captain. He strode over to the two that had heard Jesse.

"Hi," he said. "I'm Owen. I just want to say we aren't all like him. We don't think that about the Haka. Sorry. He's a ... You know?"

The taller of the two boys grinned. "No worries,

mate," he said. "I'm Kane and this is Lucas. And there's idiots in every team. We have our own. Don't worry about it."

Owen smiled.

"What do you think of the pitch then?" Lucas asked. "Not bad, eh?"

"I love it," Owen said.

"When the All Blacks are getting ready for a game in Auckland they train here," Kane said.

"Really?" Owen was thrilled at the idea of playing on the same pitch as the All Blacks. "Do you get to watch?"

Kane nodded. "Yeah. They're our heroes, totally."

"Can I ask ..." Owen said. "I'd like to know ... really, do your school do the Haka before games?"

"Course we do," Kane said.

"Fantastic." Owen grinned. "I hope I get to see it. In the final."

In fact, Owen knew that Borderlands mightn't be playing Auckland at all. Borderlands would begin against the winners of the Australian Schools Trophy, Thomastown. Auckland would then take on Cape Crusaders of South Africa. Both semi-finals would be played on the pitch here at Auckland.

Then the two semi-final winners would play each other. But not here. The final would be held in Eden Park – home of the mighty All Blacks, the New Zealand national team. It was one of the most famous rugby stadiums in the world.

THREE

On the first morning of Borderlands' stay in New Zealand, after a broken night's sleep and a steady training session, Owen and his team-mates went on a tour of Eden Park.

The tour began at the very top of the main stand. Their leader was a tall man in a white shirt, the stadium manager. He introduced himself as Steve, then waited for the boys to settle down.

"So here we are," he announced, "at Eden Park. Home of the All Blacks!"

Owen grinned. The view was amazing. A huge pitch. Four stands. Tens of thousands of seats facing into one of the world's great theatres of sport. Beyond it was the city of Auckland with the point of the Sky Tower reaching into the blue and a range of mountains in the background.

Owen could tell that Steve was very proud of his stadium. And who could blame him? But Owen could also see that at least three of his team-mates were looking at their phones – and not paying any attention.

"It's brilliant," Owen said. He wanted to show Steve that he – at least – was impressed by Eden Park. He was embarrassed that his team-mates seemed more interested in their phones. Jesse was doing it. Even Rory! He couldn't believe it.

Owen made his way towards Rory. "What are you doing?" he hissed. "We should be listening to the tour."

"They're back," Rory said.

"What?"

"The squadron. They're back home."

Now Owen understood. He felt himself cringe, ashamed to have challenged Rory like that. Their parents were home from the war. Texts were flooding in from home. There wasn't a building in the world that would impress them right now.

A little later, at the next stage of the tour, the Borderlands team were joined by another group of boys. Thomastown School from Sydney, Australia.

"And this," Steve said, "is the tunnel. One of you teams will walk down it and out onto the pitch when you play in the final in a week's time. Out of the dressing room used by the likes of Richie McCaw and Jonah Lomu."

"You Poms had best have a good look round now,"

one of the Australian players joked. "You'll not be here on Friday."

"We will be here," Jesse snapped.

"No way. This is too big a stage for you boys," another of the Australians said. "You're in the southern hemisphere now. Where the English come to lose."

Owen smiled. Aussie sledging. It always got under the skin of English players. At times like this, he felt extra proud to be Welsh.

"Like 2003?" Jesse snapped again. He stood in front of the two Australian boys so they had to stop or collide with him. "That was at your place, wasn't it? The World Cup final, I seem to remember?"

"Ancient history, mate. I'm talking about this week." The Australian boy was smiling. He had Jesse totally out-classed.

Then Steve led both teams into a supply tunnel

that ran underneath the stadium and into the home dressing room. The argument rumbled on. Owen watched Jesse carefully. He was fuming – the Australians had got to him big time. Owen just hoped that it wouldn't make Jesse mess up his game tomorrow.

FOUR

The whole Borderlands team were staying in the Auckland Grammar School boarding house, a big white wooden building that overlooked the rugby pitches. They had five dorms with four boys in each.

Owen woke the next morning long before Woody and Rory. The time difference between home and New Zealand was bothering him. His body felt sluggish and heavy, and his mind had no idea whether it was day or night. He'd been wide awake since 3 a.m. He'd passed the time reading *Calon*, the book Miss Evans had given him, then closing his eyes and kidding himself he was asleep.

Owen wanted to give the book everything he could. He knew he had to keep the momentum going if he was going to finish it, and so he was reading it in short bursts every time he got a chance. Which wasn't a problem – he was loving it. It was thrilling to find out about George North, the Millennium Stadium and how the Welsh team trained. More than that, Owen felt like he was there with them, that he was one of them.

The title of the book – *Calon* – meant "heart" in Welsh. And it made Owen's heart swell just to look at the photos, the red shirts and white shorts. Now he understood why the New Zealand boys filled their school with photos of their incredible rugby heritage.

As he drifted off again, Owen was disturbed by the sound of something outside. Footsteps. He perched on the end of his bed and stared out between the curtains. It was barely light outside.

But he could make out shadows, the shapes of people walking down towards the school. Boys wearing shorts and rugby boots, carrying towels.

They were training!

Owen checked the time: 6.15 a.m. He had to admire their dedication.

Borderlands never trained as a team before the school day started. Rory was known to sneak out at all hours with his notebook and ball to work on his kicking, but no one else would start so early.

Owen leaned out of the window to watch the squad do laps of the rugby pitches, then a series of stretches. When they finished, half an hour had gone and the sun was up.

Owen looked back into his room and saw that only one other bed had someone in it – Thomas's. So where were Woody and Rory? Owen hadn't noticed them get up.

Owen slipped out of bed and opened the door to the common area between all the boys' rooms. There were giant beanbags in one corner and a huge TV screen decorated with New Zealand rugby flags with their famous silver fern. Woody and Rory were leaning over a pool table at the other end of the room. They were both staring at Woody's iPad, which was propped up on the green felt of the table.

"What's up?" Owen whispered.

Rory looked round. "Woody's trying to Skype his dad. I've tried my mum and dad. It's early evening at home. We thought …" Rory stopped.

"No joy?" Owen asked. He could see that his friend was upset.

"No. I can't get it to connect. But it should work. I've done everything like you're meant to."

"I'm sorry," Owen said. "Maybe it's just the Wi-Fi in here."

"It's everything," Woody said. "We've not had any texts either. Just some information would be good."

"I just want to see them in the front room at home," Rory said. "You know?"

Owen nodded. But, like the stuff they'd talked about on the flight, he didn't know. And he wasn't sure what to do to help his friends.

"Erm ... do you want a cup of tea?" he asked.

And then Rory and Woody were laughing out loud. So loud Owen was worried they'd wake the other boys up.

Owen went red. "What?" he asked. "What did I say?"

Once they had stopped laughing, Woody explained. "That's what people always do. Make a cup of tea. Nine times out of ten you can't contact your parents. And there's always someone there to make a cup of tea. Yes, Owen, I'd love one. Thank you."

"Me too." Rory grinned.

Owen smiled too. At least he knew he wasn't any more useless than anyone else. He would make them some tea. That's what you did.

"Earl Grey," Woody said as Owen walked towards the kitchen.

"What?" Owen was puzzled.

"Do you have Earl Grey? Or Lapsang dodah?"

"Ermmmm." Owen wasn't sure what to say.

Rory started laughing again. Then Woody.

Owen nodded and grimaced. "I'll just take a flight to Lapsang. Get you some of that fancy tea and bring it back. Won't be long."

FIVE

That afternoon, Owen stood with his Borderlands
team-mates on the main pitch at Auckland. To his
right was their amazing club house. To his left, the
players from the Australian team were warming up.
Some of the boys were talking to Jesse across the
halfway line.

This was it.

The semi-final of the World Schools Rugby
Trophy.

Borderlands against Thomastown of Australia.

Owen breathed in and out to calm himself down.

Then he looked at his two best friends to see

how they were coping. Rory was standing with his back to the team, staring into space. Woody was too. Owen knew that wasn't right. Not right at all. In fact, the whole feel of the team wasn't right for the start of a match. Everyone was in their own world.

They're worrying about their parents, Owen thought. *And why shouldn't they? Their parents are way more important than rugby.*

But the fact remained that this was rugby. It was really important rugby. They all had to give it 100% or they might as well not have bothered flying all the way round the world to play in the tournament.

Owen looked for Jesse. He was the one who should be doing something now. He was their captain – he should be giving everyone a boost, bringing them together. He needed to make them forget their families for a couple of hours and focus on the game instead. But Owen could see that Jesse was too busy sledging the Australians. And Mr Johnson had already done his team talk in the dressing room.

So Owen decided that he should do something. He was one of the few who didn't have to worry about his mum and dad.

"Lads," he called out. "Lads!"

Only Rory and Woody looked round. No one else.

Owen decided to go for it. He shouted this time. "Lads! Gather round."

And they did. One by one, then in twos and threes, the whole Borderlands team came to stand in a semi-circle around Owen. Only Jesse and David ignored him. They were still right up on the halfway line, chest to chest with the opposition. Owen breathed in again. He decided to ignore Jesse and David. He had to talk to the team.

"I can't imagine what it's like having your mum or dad away at war," he said to them all. "I can't imagine what it's like to have them come back when you're not there, when you're on the other side of the world." Owen paused. "But I can imagine it must feel rubbish. So can I say something?"

Four lads said yes. None said no. Owen took it as permission.

"I was with you at Twickenham when we won the National Schools Trophy. I was with you when we won in Toulon. We're the European champions. And we won both those finals when your parents were fighting a war." Owen paused for a second. "I don't know how you did that. I'm amazed by what you can do."

Owen saw that the semi-circle of boys was moving into a huddle. Arms were going round shoulders. There was a grittier look in his team-mates' eyes. They were starting to behave more like they were a rugby team before a big game.

"If you could do that then," Owen went on, "I think you can do it again today. You know your parents are home or are coming home. You wish

you were there too. But you're here. And, like I said, I can't imagine it, but I know you all and I think you can do it again today."

Owen stopped. He wondered if he sounded like a fool, making this big fancy speech. But he saw that all eyes were on him. There was that gritty look of determination in those eyes. Perhaps his speech had worked.

And then – as they broke up the huddle – there was a rush of noise. The doors of Auckland Grammar School were flung open. All of a sudden, the walkways were filled with hundreds of boys pouring out of the school. The whole school stampeded down to watch the game. They filed round all sides of the pitch, and most of them massed on the concrete steps to Owen's right. The noise of their feet and their shouts was thrilling. Owen felt it and he could see all his team-mates were feeling it too. Everything had changed. The mood had gone from downcast to upbeat.

Jesse ambled over to the team huddle just as it broke up. "Are we ready, lads?" he asked.

"We're ready," Owen said.

"Ready to hammer these Australians?" Jesse grinned.

After the match, Owen reflected that two things had made the difference – had made it a remarkable game.

First, every single one of the New Zealanders were supporting Borderlands.

"I reckon they want the Aussies to lose," Woody said to Owen during a break in play. "More than wanting us to win."

"I reckon you're right."

The second thing, Owen had to admit, was Jesse.

He was a machine. He killed them.

From the very start he played the right passes to the right players at the right time. He made the right calls, spotted all the right weaknesses in the Thomastown line. Every time.

As the game went on, Owen could see that his team-mates had thrown off their tension and worries and were going for it. They were matching Jesse with the quality and precision of their play.

By half-time the score was 21–7.

By full-time, it was 49–19.

Jesse was on fire. The match let him show all his brilliance as a rugby player.

But as soon as the game was over, they all saw the bad side of Jesse. Owen watched him march over to his opposing number.

"How was that?" Jesse asked, right in the Aussie

boy's face. "How the hell was that? How about you come and watch us at Eden Park in the final? I'll get you a ticket if you like."

The Australian captain was having none of it. He put his hands square on Jesse's chest and pushed him away, hard. But Jesse had a mad look in his eyes. He was wired. So Owen made a decision. He ran over and grabbed Jesse round the chest, then pulled him back. Just before fists were about to fly.

Owen fell, Jesse on top of him, still lashing out with fists and feet.

Then Mr Johnson was there. And the referee.

The fight was over before it started.

And Borderlands were in the final of the World Schools Rugby Trophy.

SIX

"We're in the final."

"We beat the Aussies."

"We're playing at Eden Park."

The mood of the Borderlands team after the match was amazing. There were tables laid out with a post-match meal, but they were all too excited to sit and eat.

Borderlands were in the club house that overlooked the rugby pitches so that they could watch the second semi-final as guests of the home school. At one end there were huge windows looking out on the pitch. At the other was a wooden panel, which listed the names of the 51 All Blacks who had attended the school, and a framed All Blacks shirt. This place was beyond serious about rugby. There was no doubt in Owen's mind about that now.

The second semi-final was Auckland School versus Cape Crusaders of South Africa. The winners would play Borderlands in the final.

"You did well, lads," Mr Johnson said as he came into the club house. "Very well, in fact. I didn't expect us to turn them over so completely. But you did it. All credit to you. Whoever wins this match will be wary of us in the final now."

"We'll destroy them," Jesse boasted as the Kiwi and South African teams walked onto the pitch and lined up facing each other.

"I doubt that, Jesse," Mr Johnson said. "They're both great teams. Do you realise what it takes to be the best school rugby team in New Zealand or South Africa? Something very special, that's what. Something you've never come up against before. So we need to watch their every move. Like they've watched ours. They know our strengths and weaknesses. They'll be analysing those. Now we have to find out theirs."

Mr Johnson stopped and the boys all looked out of the club-house windows.

Woody nudged Owen. "Look, Auckland are going to do the Haka."

Owen watched as the Auckland boys lined up ten metres shy of the halfway line.

"Fantastic," Owen said. "I've never seen this apart from on TV."

And the Haka began. All 15 Auckland Grammar School boys were wearing black shorts and blue shirts so dark they looked black. Owen noticed Kane pacing among them, starting their Haka. He looked different to the easy-going boy Owen had spoken to the day before. He started the chant alone, pacing between two lines of his team-mates. Then, suddenly, the whole team let out a chant.

Owen felt a shiver go down his spine. Then the Auckland team squatted to put their fists to the ground, stuck their tongues out and fell to their knees. All the time they chanted in deep voices that Owen could feel vibrating in his chest, even from the side of the pitch.

Owen felt emotion and excitement course through him just watching it. He wanted Auckland to win so he could stand with the Borderlands squad and face those boys as they did the Haka at Eden Park. How could he go home and not have had that experience?

Then Jesse broke into Owen's trance. "I don't get why the South Africans just let them do it," he said. "When they do the Haka to us, we'll have an answer for it."

Typical Jesse, Owen thought. He could never let anything go without some nasty remark. The captain's bad attitude was starting to grate on Owen's nerves.

"Good idea. What did you have in mind?" an adult voice said.

Owen had to look twice to see who it was.

Mr Searle.

Owen couldn't believe that their assistant coach was agreeing with Jesse that he should disrupt the Haka. And nor did Mr Johnson.

"That is not happening," the head coach said in a sharp voice. "Do you understand me, Jesse? And, Mr Searle, please don't encourage the boys to be so disrespectful."

The mood in the club house shifted. It was a warm day, but there was a definite chill in the air now.

"Understood?" Mr Johnson repeated. He glared at Jesse before he walked over to speak to the coach of the Auckland team, who had just come into the club house. The two men walked out of the room.

Jesse didn't acknowledge Mr Johnson's glare. The minute the head coach had gone, he stood up and kicked a chair out of the way.

He looked angry, really angry.

"You don't have to do anything, sir," Jesse said to Mr Searle. "But when they do the Haka at us, we're going to walk right through them. Like the French did in the World Cup final." Then he raised his voice. "There is no way we're going to sit back and take that."

Owen cringed. He wanted to see the Haka. He wanted to admire it, not be scared of it. Jesse was threatened by its power. That much was clear. But how many people get to face the Haka before a game? Owen was sure that it would make him play harder. Some of the ideas he'd read about in *Calon* came to mind. That you should be proud of the team you play for. You should give the game everything. But – above all – you should respect the opposition. Without that respect, you'd lose and, more than that, respect was the right attitude – the only attitude.

"I'm with you, Jesse," Mr Searle said. "I've always thought the Haka was a disgrace."

"I'm a Toulon player after the final," Jesse said. "I'm leaving the school. And if Johnson wants to win the World Cup for Borderlands, he needs me in the team. He can stick it. Without me ..."

"Jesse. Outside now." Mr Johnson was back, and he was standing over them. His bulk seemed even bigger, casting a dark shadow.

Jesse had been too caught up in his own anger to notice Mr Johnson coming back.

"You too, Mr Searle," Mr Johnson said.

Owen watched Mr Johnson march to the exit. Mr Searle and Jesse had no choice but to follow in his wake.

SEVEN

The Borderlands team tried to focus on watching the second semi-final. But they knew something massive was going on in the next room. They could all hear Mr Johnson's voice coming through the wall. He wasn't shouting, but his voice was so deep that it still carried.

Miss Evans came to sit next to Owen.

"Well played today, Owen," she said. "You'll have the Welsh Rugby Union after you if you carry on like that."

"Thanks, miss."

"How's the book?"

"Good, miss," Owen said. "I'm nearly on page 100."

Miss Evans clapped her hands as if someone had scored a try. "Brilliant! 100 pages. You used to struggle to reach page 10 in any book. Now look at you."

Owen blushed. It did feel good. He was doing well and he knew it.

"It's a great book, miss," Owen said. "Thanks."

On the pitch, six minutes in, Auckland Grammar School scored a try.

Off the pitch, Owen heard a loud noise. A door slamming or a chair being kicked over. Again.

Then all the boys watched as Jesse and Mr Searle appeared outside the club house. They both walked away, through the car park and up towards the boarding house.

"What's going on?" Woody asked Owen. "Looks pretty dramatic from here."

Owen shrugged.

"I just hope he doesn't drop him," Andrew said.

"We've no chance if he does," George agreed.

"He'd never do that," Gareth said. "He'll warn him or fine him. You don't drop your best player, even if he is a ... you know."

Then the door opened and Mr Johnson appeared. His face was red with rage.

"Boys. Can I have a brief word, please?"

All eyes were on the head coach. No one was watching the other semi-final now.

"You all witnessed what went on there, I know," Mr Johnson said.

"Yes, sir," several of the boys said.

"And you also know that I gave Jesse a final warning about his conduct when we were at the European finals in Toulon."

Now no one spoke. They didn't want to take in

the logic behind what Mr Johnson was saying. But Owen knew what was coming. Jesse had his final warning in France. And now this further outrage had happened here.

"I've told Jesse and Mr Searle to pack their bags," Mr Johnson said. "They'll travel home on the next flight we can arrange for them. They'll not be staying at the boarding house with the rest of us."

"Home, sir?" asked David – Jesse's only friend on the team.

"Yes," Mr Johnson said. "Home. To Borderlands. They're off the tour. I'm sorry to do this to all of you. I know how excited you are about this tournament, and all the work you've put in. But in school and in rugby there must be discipline. Above all else. Thanks to Jesse's actions, you need to think about who your next captain will be."

"Yes, sir," the boys said.

Mr Johnson began to walk away. Then he stopped and turned.

"Look, boys ..." His tone of voice had dropped. "You will have questions. You may want to challenge me on this. But I've made my decision. I'm too angry to talk about it now and I need to watch Auckland play Cape Crusaders to see what we're going to be up against in the final. So do you. But if you want to come and talk to me about it, perhaps later this evening, I'd be open to that. Until then, enjoy the rest of the game and please don't speak to anyone else about our troubles."

With a last glance around, his face more sad than angry now, Mr Johnson left the room.

For the rest of the first half none of the boys spoke. They were all staring at the pitch. But Owen knew that they were all thinking about how they felt about Jesse being sent home. And Mr Searle too.

Some of them might be angry with Mr Johnson for being so harsh. Others might be pleased to see the back of their captain. All of them would be upset in one way or another.

Then at half-time – when the score was 34–0 to Auckland – David stood up.

"We've got problems," he said.

Two or three of the boys laughed. But they were dry, nervy laughs.

"The first problem," David said, "is that we need a captain."

"How about you?" Andrew, the Borderlands hooker, said.

"No." David shook his head. "I'm not a captain."

"What's the second problem?" Gareth asked.

David frowned. "That, at this rate, we're going to lose the final."

Owen smiled. He liked David sometimes. And he

was right about both things. The team had two huge problems that they needed to sort out. And fast.

EIGHT

The Borderlands boys met in the boarding house by the pool tables. They sprawled in a circle on giant beanbags. But no one was relaxed – they had a decision to make.

Owen had no idea who his team-mates would choose as captain. He didn't even know who he would vote for himself. Jesse had always been captain. He was an idiot, yes – but he had a very strong personality. So strong they'd never considered anyone else as captain.

Again it was David who spoke first. "Does anyone have anything to say?" he asked.

No one spoke.

"Anyone got anything to say about what happened to Jesse?" he repeated.

The question hung in the air. Owen wondered if people were too worried to say what they thought, since they knew that David was Jesse's friend. They might be scared to say that they were sick of Jesse being an idiot.

So Owen raised his hand. If they were going to sort this out, someone had to be honest and it might as well be him.

"Owen?" David said.

"I think Mr Johnson did the right thing," Owen said. "Jesse went too far. Again and again. Mr Johnson warned him, but he wouldn't stop. Mr Johnson had to punish him in the end."

"But we've got no chance in the final now," George complained. "We'll lose."

"Jesse's not our only player," Owen said. "Rory scores most of our points. We just have to play to our strengths. Get penalties."

Owen saw Rory looking straight at him. Determination was etched into his face. Owen knew he'd said the right thing.

"Good point," David said. "But we do need a new captain."

"And scrum half," Andrew said. "A decent one."

"To be honest, I'd have chosen you to be captain," Owen said to David. "But you've said you don't want it."

"I don't."

"Who votes for David?" George broke in.

Five hands went straight up. But no more.

David smiled. "See? Five? That's not enough. I'm not right for some of you. I'm not the one to be your leader."

No one spoke. They all knew he was right.

"But I can tell you who I think should be captain. And scrum half," David said. "And I bet at least ten of the hands in the room go up when I say his name."

"Who?" Gareth asked.

"Owen."

Owen stared at David in amazement. Had David really said that? Was he joking? Owen felt OK about being scrum half. He'd played scrum half for the Second XV before he made the Firsts. But captain?

"Remember when we were in France and Jesse was being so ... stupid?" David said. "Remember how the team vibe was rock bottom? Who changed that?"

"Owen," Andrew said.

"And remember at the start of this week, when everyone was feeling low just before the semi kicked off and Jesse and I were squabbling with the Aussies? Who motivated the team then?"

"Owen," three or four voices said.

Owen noticed hands going up around the room. His eyes went from team-mate to team-mate. Woody. Rory. Rhys. Thomas.

And David's hand was up now too.

"And who just said he thought we could win the final? Who's the first person to make us feel like we could do it since Jesse got himself chucked off the team?"

All hands in the room were up now.

"Well, then," David said. "There's our decision."

Owen's instinct was to say no. But he knew that if he did – and it looked like no one else was up for doing it either – then Borderlands would lose the final. He realised that he needed time to think it over.

"I have to sleep on it," Owen said. "Can I tell you in the morning? Please?"

"Sure," David said.

Owen stood up. He felt embarrassed. Everyone was looking at him.

"Right then," he said. "I'd better go to bed."

A couple of the team laughed. At least there was a better feeling in the room now.

"I'll think about it," Owen went on as he backed towards his bedroom door. "Tell you tomorrow."

This time, all his team-mates laughed.

"Sweet dreams."

"Don't let the bed bugs bite."

Owen grinned as he closed the door of the room he shared with Rory, Woody and Thomas.

His mind was all over the place. There was no chance he could think clearly about being captain. But he had to. Did he have what it took to captain a rugby team in a World Cup final?

He felt his breathing go shallow and his heart pick up a beat. He needed to calm himself down.

Then Owen saw his book. *Calon.*

He'd read that. Then sleep. He could make his mind up in the morning.

NINE

Owen climbed into bed and reached for *Calon*. He took out the card that he was using as a bookmark and looked at it. It was a note from Miss Evans.

Enjoy. Be inspired. *Cael y Calon*.

Half an hour later he was still reading. About Wales winning the Grand Slam. About Sam Warburton, one of the great Welsh captains. About what it took to be a world-class rugby player.

Then, before he knew it, it was morning. Light was coming in through the curtains. Outside he could hear the strange high-pitched whooping sounds of a bird he'd never heard before. And his face was pressed on a hard surface.

Owen looked down to see what he'd been sleeping on.

His book.

It was all he could do not to laugh.

It was still half dark in the bedroom, so Owen got dressed and went out, in the hope he wouldn't wake the others.

Outside he laughed a proper laugh. Something huge had happened.

He'd fallen asleep reading his book.

Owen had never fallen asleep reading a book before. He could feel his heart beating faster just at the thought of it. He'd not given up, got bored, found it too hard or stopped because his mind couldn't go on working out all the words. He'd stopped because he had fallen asleep. But he could remember every word he'd read as he tried to keep his eyes open. About the Grand Slam win. The stadium, the players, the pace and energy of each game. It was all so vivid that he'd felt like he was there with the Welsh players. He found it hard to believe a book could make him feel that way.

Owen looked at his watch. It was six in the morning. He was suddenly really hungry, so he wandered into the dining room of the boarding house. He assumed he would be the first one there.

But he wasn't. Miss Evans was already there.

"Hello, Owen," she said.

"Hi, miss."

"Can't sleep?" she asked.

"No," Owen said. "But I've got something to tell you."

"What's that?"

"The book you gave me. *Calon*. I love it. It's giving me a real lift. I reckon I should take it on the pitch with me at the final. It's that good, miss."

As Owen and Miss Evans ate, the Auckland students started to file in and sit at their regular tables. None of the other Borderlands players were up yet.

"Miss?" Owen said.

"Yes, Owen."

"They've asked me to be captain."

"Who has?" Miss Evans asked.

"The team. All of them."

Miss Evans put down her coffee cup. "And?"

Owen hesitated. He'd wanted to talk to Miss Evans because he thought she could help persuade him to do it.

But that was a mistake.

Now that he'd opened his mouth, he realised that

he felt so good and so strong about reading *Calon* that he felt good and strong about himself in every way.

It was a weird feeling, but the book had given him heart.

Just like Miss Evans had written in her card.

Just like the title of the book.

"I'm going to say yes," Owen told Miss Evans. "I'm going to captain Borderlands in the final."

TEN

That morning the Borderlands team played at being tourists. Mr Johnson had arranged a day trip to the New Zealand Rugby Museum. A bus came for them after breakfast.

Before the bus set off, Owen told the others that he would be happy to be their captain.

The three cheers that followed made him blush.

But he made sure he looked each of them in the eye. In *Calon* he'd read that's what Sam Warburton did in the huddle before matches. If he was going to be like any captain, he'd be like him.

The bus took them to the airport.

They travelled from Auckland to Palmerston North in a small plane that flew low enough for Owen to see every inch of the rugged landscape of New Zealand. The pilot told them about the extinct volcanoes they were travelling over and how a huge fault in the earth's structure ran through a cross section of the country, which is what made the New Zealand landscape so remarkable. He pointed out lands that belonged to the Maori people and he spoke about the country's history before Europeans arrived. He even explained about the Haka and how it was a war dance used by the Maoris to prepare themselves for battle.

Owen loved hearing about New Zealand. The pilot brought his country to life and Owen was really looking forward to the rugby museum by the time they landed 40 minutes later.

The museum wasn't big. There was a set of

display cases around a netted area where some of the boys took part in kicking and scrum challenges. The displays were full of balls and shirts and images showing 150 years of rugby in New Zealand.

Owen was drawn like a magnet to the Haka display. He was worried that his interest in the New Zealand pre-match ritual was becoming an obsession. But he couldn't help himself.

He read that the Haka had first been done by a warrior chief who was fleeing his enemies. When he'd turned and performed a Haka, they had all run away.

But it wasn't the story that did it for Owen. It was listening to the Haka that sent a shiver down his spine as he faced the large photo of the All Blacks delivering it. It was like nothing he'd ever heard. Not like poetry. Not like music. Not like shouting or singing. It was unique.

Mr Johnson was standing behind Owen. "How does it make you feel?" he asked.

"Excited," Owen admitted. "I like it. I know I'm meant to be intimidated, but ..."

"No." Mr Johnson shook his head. "You've got the right attitude. The Haka is a war dance. The Maoris did it before they went into battle. To fire themselves up. To warm up. They use every muscle they have when they do it. To prepare to fight. You can take it two ways. You can be afraid of it. Or you can be inspired by it."

"I'm inspired, sir," Owen said. "Definitely."

"Good." Mr Johnson lowered his voice. "Because I think Jesse was intimidated by it."

Owen said nothing.

"I'm pleased they chose you, Owen," Mr Johnson said at last. "And I'm pleased you accepted. Miss Evans told me about your chat this morning."

"Yes, sir."

"You've done well. I'm proud of you."

"Thank you, sir."

There was another pause. Then Mr Johnson lowered his voice for a second time. "I want you to know that I would have chosen you too, Owen," he said.

Owen looked at his rugby master. "Really, sir?"

"Really, Owen. I think you've already proved you'll be a great captain. I'll ask you to speak to the boys about the Haka before the final, if I may?"

"You may, sir," Owen said with a grin.

After the museum, the boys had an hour to explore Palmerston North. Most of them hung around a large park by a square of shops with a war memorial at its centre.

Owen noticed that Woody, Rory and some of the others were in a cafe on the edge of the park. They sat outside with their iPads and their phones out.

Owen knew they were trying to contact home. But he also knew that they had no chance. It was 4 a.m. back home. His team-mates must be desperate if they were trying now.

And when he saw them shuffle from the cafe to the bus, he could see how dejected they were.

Not good. Dejection was not what he wanted his team to be feeling.

As captain, he'd have to do something to lift their spirits. Or Borderlands would have no chance of performing at their best in the final of the World Schools Trophy, let alone winning it.

ELEVEN

Two days later, the bus carrying the Borderlands players drew up at Eden Park. It went in a large iron gate and under the main stand, then it passed into the service tunnel. Owen gazed at the stands and turf and Eden Park signs. He couldn't quite believe they were going to play here.

All the players were aware that Mr Johnson was watching them from the front of the bus.

"This is how teams like Australia and England and Wales arrive here for a match," he said. "So you deserve to come in the same way."

They came to a halt and Owen led his team off

the bus. As he did, he noticed that everyone stole a glance out along the tunnel at the green of the pitch, before they turned towards the dressing rooms. These were the same dressing rooms they had seen on the tour. Except, this time, there were 15 yellow and blue Borderlands shirts where the shirts of Richie McCaw and Jonah Lomu had hung.

"Let the lads settle in first," Mr Johnson said in a low voice to Owen as they went into the dressing room. "Then I'll do my team talk. And you say a few words too. OK?"

"OK," Owen said. Then he watched his team-mates, judging their mood. Some were trying out the warm-up bikes at the far end of the dressing room, loosening their muscles. Others were using the loos.

"I just peed where Dan Carter peed," Rahim said.

"How do you know?" Danny asked. "He might not have used the one you did."

"I peed in all three," Rahim replied.

Owen smiled as several of the Borderlands team laughed. He was pleased. There was a good relaxed feel among them. If they were going to stand any chance in this match, they needed to be relaxed.

It was the final of the World Schools Rugby Trophy. There was no bigger game than this for a schoolboy.

Just before Borderlands were due to go out, Mr Johnson called the team together.

"I'll keep this short, lads," he said. "We've already talked tactics. We've studied their play, decided on a plan. You're about to play in the final of the World Schools Trophy. At Eden Park. This is, without doubt, the biggest game of your lives so far."

The coach paused so the players could take in his words.

"You will be nervous," Mr Johnson went on. "And you should be nervous. I want you to be nervous. But you're relaxed too, settled in yourselves. I overheard Rahim joking just now. A magic moment, no doubt." There was laughter in his voice. "But one day Dan Carter was here in this dressing room on his debut for the All Blacks. He will have been nervous that day too."

Mr Johnson smiled.

"But you can be sure that once he was on the pitch, he will have done what every player must do when they play here. He will have given it everything. You can be nervous, relaxed, laughing, feeling sick. You can be all those things and more, and you can – and must – give it everything on the pitch. I believe in you, in Borderlands. And I know that you'll give it your all."

Mr Johnson stepped to one side and waved for Owen to stand up.

"We all know there was trouble about Jesse and the Haka," the coach added. "His attitude was wrong. But I think your captain has it right. So I'd like to ask Owen to prepare us for the Haka. Owen?"

This was it.

Owen tried to smile, but his face didn't quite work. He knew he was their captain, but it was hard to take it in when someone called him that.

He struggled to level out the shake in his voice. "I just wanted to say ..." he said, then started again. "I just wanted to say that when we were at the museum a few days ago, I spent a lot of time staring at that Haka display. Who else saw it?"

Owen watched as every player's hand went up. He saw their faces as one. They looked serious. They were listening.

"When I looked at that display, I was afraid I'd be nervous facing the Haka today," Owen said. "But then I felt something else. The Haka is about to be performed to us – at Eden Park. There is nothing about the Haka we need to worry about."

Owen could sense that he was beginning to speak faster.

"And that's because we've earned the right to face down the Haka," he went on. "We're one of the two best school rugby teams on the planet. It's our right to face the Haka. It's our right to draw power and energy from it. And it's our right to be playing in the World Schools final. Am I right? Am I right?"

The roar that went up was so loud that Owen was sure the Auckland boys would have heard it in their dressing room.

Good, he thought. *That's no bad thing.*

TWELVE

The noise of the roar from the Borderlands team was nothing compared to the noise of the crowd. Owen was the first to see why it was so loud. The two stands running the length of the pitch were as good as full. There had to be 30,000 people watching.

Owen could see that some of his team-mates were shocked by the noise and size of the crowd.

"Let's focus, lads," he shouted. "Line up. Face the home team."

He wanted them to forget about the crowd as soon as they could.

In their dark blue shirts and black shorts, the

New Zealand champions could have been mistaken for the All Blacks themselves. They stood strong against the black letters spelling out "EDEN PARK" on the stand behind them.

Owen had said everything he needed to say about the Haka. He just hoped it would give his team-mates strength, not the opposite.

Then it began. Kane from Auckland walked up and down among his team-mates, whipping them into a frenzy. The sounds of the Maori language filled the stadium, echoing from stand to stand.

To Owen it was amazing to watch their faces, their staring eyes, their posture as they performed their dance. He could feel a real surge of power coming from the Kiwi boys. But it wasn't a power that was working against him and his team. It was a power that seemed to fill the stadium, pouring into both teams and the huge crowd too. The roar they gave up at the end of the Haka was deafening.

Ka mate, ka mate!	*It is death! It is death!*
Ka ora, ka ora!	*It is life! It is life!*
Ka mate! Ka mate!	*It is death!* *It is death!*
Ka ora! Ka ora!	*It is life!* *It is life!*
Tēnei te tangata pūhuruhuru	*This is the hairy man*
Nāna nei i tiki mai whakawhiti te rā.	*Who fetched the sun and* *made it shine.*
Ā upane! Ka upane!	*One step upward!* *Another step upward!*
Ā upane, ka upane – whiti te ra!	*An upward step, another* *upward step – the sun* *shines!*

Auckland kicked off, a high ball that fell to Rory, who made a perfect catch, then passed it ten metres across to Woody.

Woody charged. This was his first time going at the Auckland defence, and Owen knew he would want to let their opponents know he was there. Two Auckland forwards came in at him hard. They seemed to know he was the man to stop. And they did stop him. But not until he'd gained eight metres.

Woody turned and set the ball down for Owen.

Owen picked the ball up and played it low to Sunil. Four phases later, Borderlands were ten metres out.

Owen was thrilled. He loved the fast tempo Borderlands had begun with. They hadn't given the home team a minute to settle. He'd planned to build up points slowly all game, earning penalties, relying on Rory's kicking. But the speed and energy with which Borderlands were attacking was too exciting to hold back.

Owen took the ball from a driving maul and span it out to Woody, who had already gathered momentum from deep. The momentum was so great that he took his two forwards with him. And now he had Andrew and Gareth behind him, pushing their shoulders at him, another driving maul, soon joined by David and Duncan. All the weight of the Borderlands pack focused behind Woody.

The force of it was irresistible.

Woody was over, his hands reaching down, placing the ball over the line.

A try.

Owen punched the air. It was hard to believe Borderlands had scored so quickly: 5–0 within three minutes. Then 7–0 after Rory's conversion. A fantastic way to show Auckland that they could compete.

But Owen knew he had to focus his troops. They had to keep their heads. They'd not faced the Auckland attack yet. And the thought of that made him very wary indeed.

Auckland kicked off again. Rhys took the ball this time, just before the Auckland forwards took him down. Owen was behind Sunil and ready to get the ball to the other backs. But this time his pass fell short.

His mistake.

And he knew it.

Borderlands had lost possession.

Now they were under pressure on their 22. Now they would see what the Auckland attack was like.

Right away, Auckland exerted intense pressure. It was so intense that Owen could tell that all the Borderlands boys were struggling. He cursed himself. They were deep in their own half and deep in trouble less than a minute after scoring the opening try.

With the ball for the first time, Auckland were ruthless. Their centres piled into Borderlands and cut through their defence. One pass, another pass, then a third, and they sliced through the Borderlands back line.

Try.

An all too easy try. An easy conversion too.

7–7.

Then eight minutes later – after a handling error from Rhys after a scrum – another try. Not converted. 12–7 to Auckland.

This went on all first half. Borderlands would defend well enough and attack well enough too. But the attack always seemed to break down at a key moment. Owen knew why it was happening. Those key moments were the kind of moments where Jesse would have sent out a killer pass.

Then, when Borderlands were on the back foot, they would crumble. The Auckland team would make ten or more metres and Owen would see panic on the faces of his team-mates. His own idea of a game based on building up penalty kicks was impossible to deliver in this frenzy of attack.

By half-time it was 29–7. Five tries against. Two converted.

As he led his players off at half-time, Owen stared at the ground. He'd never felt so dejected or defeated. What was he going to say now?

He was meant to be the captain. The leader.

How could he bring his team back from this so that they could turn it round in the second half? How could he bring his team round from the stark truth that without Jesse as scrum half and captain, Borderlands were clumsy, error-prone and facing a severe thrashing?

THIRTEEN

Back under the huge main stand of Eden Park, Owen stood at the head of the tunnel and waited for his team-mates to leave the pitch for half-time. He patted each one of them on the back and said "Well tried" to them all.

They had tried hard.

Very hard.

Even so, they'd been utterly out-classed by Auckland Grammar School. 29–7 said it all.

As he came off, Owen looked up at the main stand and tried to think of the words he could say to his team-mates. What was a captain meant to say at half-time when the opposition had as good as won the game? Should he fire them up to try to make an astonishing comeback? Or should he suggest they just play for self-respect and avoid a cricket score?

This was a nightmare. Why had he let them choose him as captain?

He felt hopeless. Helpless. Horrible.

As he gazed into space, punishing himself, Owen saw a line of men and women file into two rows of seats not far from the front of the main stand. They were all dressed in blue. He looked again. RAF blue. Then he saw one of them waving to him, then three more. Then the whole group was waving at him.

Owen waved back and laughed. He could see Rory's mum and dad. And Woody's dad. Plus several other adults that he knew were the parents of some of his team-mates. As he waved at them, he saw what had happened. The RAF had flown the parents out to New Zealand. They'd come to Eden Park directly from the Central Asian Republic. They'd missed the first half, but they were here now.

That was why Woody and Rory had been unable to contact their parents.

Now Owen knew what he had to say.

He marched under the stand to his dressing room and asked Mr Johnson to step outside.

"I need a word, sir," Owen said.

"Owen, don't worry," Mr Johnson told him. "Auckland are a superb outfit. You're not to blame ..."

Owen shook his head. "No, sir. This is more important."

Mr Johnson looked puzzled. "What is it?"

"The parents. They're here."

"Fantastic," Mr Johnson said. "I didn't think they'd make it."

"You knew?" Owen said.

"I knew there was a plan."

"But you didn't want to disappoint the lads?"

"That's right. In case they didn't get here on time."

"So shall I tell them?" Owen asked. "It might affect the second half."

Mr Johnson nodded. "It will affect the second half, Owen. But this is your call, son. You're captain. What's your gut feeling?"

Owen thought about it for a moment. What was best for the boys whose mums and dads were out there, back from war? And what was best for the rest of the team? For their hopes of turning the game round?

Mr Johnson was waiting for an answer. Owen had a clear idea of what it was.

"We take the team out now," he said. "Spend five minutes talking to the parents in their stand. Then five minutes refocusing for the second half."

Mr Johnson smiled. "That's a fine idea, Owen. Go in there and tell them. Lead them out."

Owen went into the dressing room and asked his players to come back out onto the pitch.

"Why?" Gareth asked. "We need to regroup. Not spend more time out there."

"Trust me," Owen said. "Come on."

There were mutterings behind Owen as they walked back out along the tunnel and onto Eden Park. Once they were on the pitch, Owen turned the team round and pointed at the two rows of RAF personnel. Their faces were a picture.

"You've got five minutes to talk to your parents," Owen said. "No more. And don't go into the stands. Stay out here. Then I want you back on the pitch. I need you focused. We've a second half to play."

Owen knew he would never understand what it meant to have a parent away at war and in danger.

He'd never understand what it was like not knowing when – or if – they were coming home.

But as he watched his team-mates reach out to their mums and dads, and the parents jump down to grab their kids, he had a decent idea.

The other fans in the stadium fell quiet so that the Borderlands boys could talk to their parents. They seemed to know what was going on.

Owen smiled and folded his arms.

No matter the score right now, it felt good to be a captain.

FOURTEEN

The second half was different to the first.
Borderlands had a renewed spirit and a flow to their
game. It paid off within five minutes.

Owen took the ball from the back of the scrum
25 metres out and fed it to Woody. Woody didn't
battering-ram the Auckland defence – instead he
played a long pass out to George on the wing and
took the Auckland back line by surprise. Thomas
charged over, managing to keep his feet just inside
the line.

Try. Converted by Rory.

29–14.

Now the gap between the teams didn't look so wide.

The game didn't feel like such a lost cause.

But it did when Auckland broke through on 49 minutes. And again on 67 minutes. One try converted. One missed.

In between, Woody had scored a single try. And Rory had missed the conversion.

With only four minutes left, Owen eyed the scoreboard. 41–19.

The game was lost and it had been lost by the end of the first half. He knew it. Everyone knew it. Borderlands would not be world champions.

But Owen knew there was one thing that would make his team feel less bad about defeat. They could still win the second half. It was a target, a focus. That would make a difference to the team. And to the parents who had missed the first half anyway.

If Borderlands could score once, then the parents would have seen Borderlands score more points than Auckland. That would feel like a victory of sorts.

Owen had seen the parents amassing near the tunnel area, ready to run onto the pitch as soon as the whistle blew for the end of the game. They couldn't wait to get hold of their sons.

One score would do it. A penalty. A try. Or a drop goal. One score that would make the parents – and their sons – happy.

So, during a break in play – when Auckland were bringing on a sub – Owen spoke to Woody and Rory. He could tell his friends were shattered and keen for the game to end so they could see their parents.

"We can win this half," Owen said.

"OK," both his friends said. They were breathing deeply, hands on hips.

"The three of us need to set it up," Owen said.

"I'll feed you, Woody, off this scrum. We're 40 metres out. Woody, make as much ground as you can. I'll be behind you. Push the ball back to me, then, Rory, you stay centre of the field, ready for a pass. Then drop it. OK?"

"OK," both his friends said again.

Then Owen wound his pack up, shouting at them to win the scrum, to win it for the parents.

Borderlands took the Auckland pack by surprise with their power – and they won it easily.

Owen waited until he could see Woody charging towards him, then he tossed the ball crisply into his path.

Woody was running at pace, but he was brought down having made five metres. It was a great effort. Owen reached for the ball, hesitated and saw that Rory was in place. Forty metres out. A long way for an under-15 to score a drop goal.

But Owen had faith.

He plucked the ball from the ground and spun it out to Rory.

Rory took it cleanly, dropped the ball and fired it high towards the far stand of Eden Park. It sailed in between the posts. Perfect.

41–22.

Anyone coming into Eden Park at the end of the game, who saw 20 or so adults run onto the pitch and grab their sons, would think that the team in yellow and blue had just won the World Cup. If they'd looked at the faces of the Borderlands team, they'd have thought the same. Huge grins. Tears. Hugs. Arms draped round each other.

They would have also thought that Auckland Grammar School were the losers, the way they stood and applauded Borderlands, paying respect to the team and their parents.

But the truth was something completely different.

Owen watched Woody's dad sprinting across the grass to grab his son. And Rory going the other way to leap at both of his parents.

He knew how intense the emotions were that his friends would be feeling now. He'd been with them every day for the months that they'd had to be apart from their parents. He'd talked to them, given them space and tried, at times, to use rugby to distract them.

Owen didn't need to do that now.

Borderlands had lost the final of the World Schools Rugby Trophy.

But it didn't matter.

They had just won so much more.

FIFTEEN

After Borderlands had stood and clapped the Auckland team as they went up to receive the trophy, Owen jogged over to Kane. "Storming," he said. "Congratulations."

"Cheers, mate. That was a blinding second half."

"Thanks," Owen said with a grin. "How about we swap shirts?"

Kane nodded. "Love to."

The two boys swapped shirts, shook hands, then Owen watched Kane go off to celebrate with his team-mates.

He felt proud to have played against Auckland –

and to have Kane's shirt. He felt elated like never before. He was looking forward.

To next season.

To playing more rugby.

And to tonight – after the post-match party – when he would read the last few pages of *Calon*. He would finish it and then think which book he would like to read next.